KT-592-017

Contents

The Citadel

turned on or before
below.

A. J. CRONIN

Level 5

Retold by Norman Wymer
Series Editors: Andy Hopkins and Jocelyn Potter

Pearson Education Limited
Edinburgh Gate, Harlow,
Essex CM20 2JE, England
and Associated Companies throughout the world.

ISBN 0 582 41926 3

First published in the Longman Simplified English Series 1963
First published in the Longman Fiction Series 1993
This adaptation first published in 1996
by arrangement with Victor Gollancz Ltd
Third impression 1998
This edition first published 1999
Second impression 2001

This edition copyright © Penguin Books Ltd 1999
Cover design by Bender Richardson White

Set in 11/14pt Bembo
Printed in Spain by Mateu Cromo, S.A.Pinto (Madrid)

Published by Pearson Education Limited in association with
Penguin Books Ltd, both companies being subsidiaries of Pearson Plc

For a complete list of the titles available in the Penguin Readers series please write to your local
Pearson Education office or to: Marketing Department, Penguin Longman Publishing,
5 Bentinck Street, London W1M 5RN.

Introduction

Archibald Joseph Cronin was born in Dunbartonshire, Scotland in 1896. From the time of his father's death, when he was only seven years old, Cronin was brought up by his mother's family. He studied medicine at the University of Glasgow while working in a mental hospital in order to earn enough money to live on. During World War I he was a surgeon in the Royal Navy, and he finally completed his studies in 1919.

Cronin's first job after the war was as a medical helper in a small Scottish village. From 1921 to 1924 he practised medicine in South Wales. He then became a medical officer responsible for mines, and did research into work-related diseases in the coal industry. In 1926 he opened a medical practice in London, but he had to give this up in 1930 because of his own ill-health. His illness forced him to rest for several months, and he took his family to stay on a quiet farm in the Highlands of Scotland, where he wrote his first book. It was an immediate success, and Cronin was soon able to make a living from his writing. Towards the end of his life Cronin lived mostly in the United States and in Switzerland, and it was in Montreux, Switzerland that he died in 1981.

Cronin's first book was *Hatter's Castle*. This appeared in 1931 and tells the story of a Scottish hatmaker who is driven by the idea that he really belongs to an upper-class family. The book was an immediate success, and was made into a film in 1941. One of Cronin's best works is *The Stars Look Down* (1935), which is set in a mining area in the north of England between the years 1903 and 1933. It tells the story of a man who leaves the mines and finally becomes a Member of Parliament, and it gained Cronin an international readership. *The Citadel* appeared in 1937, and was followed by *The Keys of the Kingdom*, a highly religious book about a man who travels to China to teach people about the Roman Catholic faith. Later works include *Shannon's Way* (1948), *The Judas Tree* (1961) and *A Song of Sixpence* (1964), the story of a mother's struggle to care for her son after his father's death. A popular British television series called *Dr Finlay's Casebook* was based on Cronin's early stories of the lives of Scottish doctors. Cronin's stories show the interest that he took in the details of places and of people's lives. His best books are based closely on his own experience, which brings them to life for the reader.

The Citadel draws on Cronin's time as a doctor, and a number of the situations in the book are taken directly from Cronin's own experiences. The question of safety in mines was very much in his readers' minds at the time. In September 1934, 262 people were killed in an accident at a Welsh mine. But what really called attention to the book when it appeared was its sharp criticism of the weaknesses of the British medical profession. It shows how unprepared young doctors were for treating the sick when they finished their medical training. Dr Manson is completely out of his depth when he has to deal with real patients for the first time, and much of the illness that he is expected to cure is in fact caused by the poor living conditions of his patients. The book also draws attention to the shortage of hospitals, and the poor quality of those that there were. But it is the inequality that existed in the treatment of the rich and the poor that particularly shocks the young doctor. Cronin himself clearly felt very strongly about this. The poor are given worthless advice and useless medicines; the rich are often made to pay for the best possible treatment, even when they are not really ill. But the message that comes across at the end is one of hope as Manson begins to find ways of overcoming the misery and difficulties that he finds. And protests such as Cronin's must surely have played their part in making Britain, in 1948, the first country in the world to operate a National Health Service.

When the story begins, the newly qualified doctor Andrew Manson arrives in the town of Drineffy in South Wales to take up his first job. He is young and very keen, but he soon discovers that his professional life will not be easy. His first shock comes when he meets Dr Page, for whom he will be working, and finds that he can expect little help from him. As he starts to understand the problems of the existing medical system, he becomes more and more determined to change it. He makes enemies in the process, but gains some friends too. These include Philip Denny, whose behaviour Manson at first finds shocking and unacceptable, and the attractive young schoolteacher Christine Barlow. The reader feels sympathy for the young doctor as he struggles against the system, and often with himself, in a brave attempt to do what he believes is right.

Chapter 1   The New Doctor

Late one October afternoon in the year 1924 a badly dressed young man looked eagerly out of the window of his railway carriage in the almost empty train. Manson had been travelling all day, but the last stage of his long journey to South Wales moved him to great excitement as he thought of the post, his first as a doctor, that he was about to take up in this, wild country.

Outside, the rain beat down between the mountains on either side of the railway line. The tops of the mountains were hidden by a grey sky; and their sides, which contained many coal mines, looked black and cold. Night was falling and no trees, no grass could be seen. At a bend in the railway line, a bright red light from an iron works suddenly came into view, lighting up a number of men who were working with all their strength. At once, a sense of power filled the mountain valley. Manson drew a deep breath. He felt an added call to effort, a sudden hope and promise for the future.

It was dark when, half an hour later, his train reached Drineffy. He had arrived at last. Manson jumped from the train and hurried out of the station.

In the street, an old man in dirty clothes looked at him carefully, and asked: 'Are you Dr Page's new man?'

'That's right. Manson's my name – Andrew Manson.'

'Hm! Mine's Thomas. I've got the carriage here. Get in!'

Manson climbed into the carriage, which was badly in need of repair; and they drove in silence through several streets of small, dirty houses. Old Thomas, whose body gave off an unpleasant smell, kept looking strangely at Manson. At last he said: 'You've only just left college, eh?'

Andrew smiled.

'I thought so!' old Thomas said, scornfully. 'The last man left ten days ago. They never stay for long!'

'Why?' Andrew asked, trying to hide his anxiety.

'The work's too hard, for one reason.'

'And what are the other reasons?'

'You'll soon find out!'

After leaving the centre of the town, they drove across some rough ground near a coal mine, and then up a narrow, stony road to a house close to the rows of small miners' houses.

'This is the house,' said Thomas, stopping the horse.

Andrew got out of the carriage. The next minute the front door was thrown open, and he was welcomed by a tall woman of about fifty.

'Well! Well! You must be Dr Manson. Come inside. I'm Dr Page's sister, Miss Page. I *am* pleased to see you!' she said with a friendly smile. 'Our last man was of no use; but I'm sure that I can trust you. Come with me, and I will show you your bedroom.'

Andrew's room was small and cold, with very little furniture. Andrew looked round the unwelcoming room and remarked politely: 'This looks very comfortable, Miss Page.'

She smiled. 'Yes, I think that you will be comfortable. Now come and meet the Doctor.' She paused, and then added awkwardly: 'I can't remember whether I told you in my letter that the Doctor is not well at the moment.'

Andrew looked at her in sudden surprise.

'Oh, it's nothing serious!' she said quickly. 'He'll soon be fit again.'

She led Andrew to the end of the passage, where she opened a door and called out to her brother: 'Here's Dr Manson, Edward.'

As Andrew entered the hot bedroom, which smelt of sickness, Edward Page turned slowly in his bed. He was a big man of perhaps sixty, with tired eyes and an expression of great suffering on his face. The light of the oil lamp, shining on to his bed, showed that one half of his face was stiff and lifeless. The left side of his body had no strength or feeling at all. These signs of a long and most serious illness gave Andrew a shock. There was an awkward silence.

'I hope that you won't find the work here too hard,' Dr Page remarked, speaking slowly and with difficulty. 'You're very young!'

'I'm twenty-four, sir,' Andrew answered. 'But I like work,' he added quickly.

Page looked at Andrew and said in a tired voice: 'I hope that you'll stay.'

'Goodness! What a thing to say!' cried Miss Page.

She smiled at Andrew, and then led him downstairs to supper. As Andrew followed her, he felt worried. No mention of Page's illness had been made when he applied for the post; but the doctor was so ill that he would never be fit to work again. Andrew asked himself why his sister had kept this fact secret.

'You're lucky, Doctor,' Miss Page remarked as they went into the dining room. 'There will be no surgery for you tonight. Jenkins has attended to it.'

'Jenkins?'

'He mixes the medicines. He's a useful man – prepared to do anything. He's been acting for the doctor and attending to all the patients during these last ten days.'

Andrew again looked at her in surprise. Was this how country doctors ran their practices?

Miss Page rang a bell; and a servant with a pale face brought in the supper, looking quickly at Andrew as she entered.

'Come along, Annie,' cried Miss Page. 'This is Dr Manson.'

Annie did not answer. She served Andrew with a small piece of cold meat, which he ate without tasting it. During the meal, Miss Page was silent. Then she sat back in her chair and described

3

in a friendly manner the medical system at Drineffy.

'All our patients are miners,' she explained. 'The Mining Company has three doctors on its lists, each of whom employs a younger doctor to help him. Dr Page now employs you, and Dr Nicholls employs a shameful man called Denny. And then there's Dr Bramwell. Each miner chooses which of the three doctors he wishes to see in times of illness; and the Company pays part of his wages each week to the doctor whom he has chosen. The doctor gives a fair share of this money to his helper and keeps the rest for himself.'

She stopped and looked at Andrew.

'I think I understand the system, Miss Page,' he said.

'Well!' She gave a short laugh. 'All that you must remember is that you are working for Dr Page. Never forget that!'

She looked at the clock, and then quickly rose from her chair. Her manner suddenly changed.

'There's a woman ill at Number 7, Glydar Place. Her husband sent for the doctor a long time ago. You had better go round there immediately,' she ordered Andrew.

Chapter 2   Fever

Andrew went out at once. He was eager to begin. This was his first case! It was still raining as he crossed the black, rough ground and made his way to the main street. Darkly, as he walked, the dirty town took shape before him. Shops and ugly churches, large and cold, filled the street. The sense of being buried deep in the valley of the mountains made Andrew tremble. There were few people about. Beyond the shops and churches, on both sides of the street, were rows and rows of houses; and at the far end of the town, lighting up the watery sky, were the Drineffy mine workings. Andrew reached Number 7, Glydar Place. He took a

4

deep breath and then knocked at the door.

He was admitted at once to the kitchen, where the patient lay in bed. She was a young woman, the wife of a miner named Williams. As Andrew went over to her bed, he suddenly felt a great sense of responsibility. He was alone. He must find out what was wrong with the woman and cure her – with no other doctor to advise him.

While the husband waited and watched in the cold, dark room, Andrew examined the woman with great care. He could see that she was ill – very ill. But what was the cause of her illness? Andrew could not discover the answer. He felt very anxious. His first case! He must not make a mistake. He examined the patient a second time, but he still did not know what was wrong with her. At last, he turned to her husband, and asked: 'Did she have a cold?'

'Yes, Doctor – three or four days ago,' Williams answered eagerly.

Andrew, trying to appear confident, said cheerfully: 'Then I'll soon make her better. Come to the surgery in half an hour. I'll give you a bottle of medicine for her.'

He quickly left the house and walked back in the rain to the surgery, an old wooden building in Page's garden. He lit the gaslight and walked up and down the room, trying to think of any illness from which the woman might be suffering. He knew that it was not really her cold that had made her ill; she had something far worse wrong with her. Feeling very annoyed with himself for his stupidity, he took some bottles from a shelf, and mixed a medicine.

He had just finished this, and was putting the woman's name and address on to the bottle, when the surgery bell rang. Before Andrew could answer this, the door opened, and a short, powerful man of about thirty walked in, followed by a dog. The man, who wore an old suit of clothes and dirty shoes, looked

Andrew up and down.

At last, he spoke. 'I saw a light in your window as I was passing by. So I decided to come in and welcome you. I'm Denny – employed by the great Dr Nicholls.'

Philip Denny lit his pipe, threw the match on to the floor, and walked forward. He picked up the bottle of medicine, smelt it, and then put it down again.

'Excellent!' he said. 'So you've begun the good work already! Medicine every three hours! The usual nonsense: when in doubt, give medicine!'

There was silence in the wooden building. Suddenly Denny laughed. 'Why have you come here?' he asked.

By this time, Andrew's temper was rising. He answered angrily: 'I want to turn Drineffy into a famous medical centre!'

Again Denny laughed. 'Clever, clever, my dear Doctor!' Then suddenly his manner changed. 'Listen, Manson,' he said, 'there are one or two things about this place that you ought to know. The medical system at Drineffy is very bad. There's no hospital, nor anything else that a doctor needs. The place is so unhealthy that people often die of fever – usually through drinking the bad water. Page was a good doctor, but he's a sick man and will never work again. Nicholls, my employer, thinks only about making money; and Bramwell, the other doctor in the area, knows nothing. And I – I drink too much. I think that's all. Come, Hawkins, we'll go.'

He called the dog and moved heavily towards the door. There he paused, took another look at the bottle of medicine, and then added: 'I advise you to consider typhoid fever in Glydar Place.'

The door closed noisily; and Denny and the dog disappeared into the wet darkness.

Andrew slept badly that night. Denny's remark had raised another doubt in his mind. Was it typhoid? As he lay in bed through the long night, Andrew asked himself if he knew

6

anything at all about the profession of medicine.

Next morning, he ate his breakfast quickly, and then went to the surgery. Jenkins was already there, mixing the medicines.

'There's no need to come here so early, Doctor,' he said. 'I can give the men their medicines and sick notes. It is not necessary for you to see them.'

'Thank you, but I wish to see them,' Andrew answered coldly. He paused and then asked quickly: 'What are you putting into those bottles?'

Jenkins smiled. 'Water, Doctor. I colour the water to make it look like medicine. The patients don't know. They think it makes them better.'

After the morning surgery, Andrew drove with old Thomas to Glydar Place. He called at Number 7, and then visited six other houses where people were now complaining of headaches and sickness. In each case, Andrew found definite signs of fever. He realized with sudden fear that the fever was already spreading. He decided that he must speak to Dr Page at once.

'Dr Page, what's the best thing to do with cases of typhoid fever?' he asked.

Page replied with closed eyes: 'Fever has always been difficult to deal with. I advise you to telephone Griffiths, the Area Medical Officer.' He paused. 'But I'm afraid that he's not very helpful.'

Andrew ran down to the hall and telephoned Griffiths.

'Hullo! Hullo! Is that Dr Griffiths?'

After a short silence, a man's voice answered: 'Who wants him?'

'This is Manson of Drineffy. I work for Dr Page. I have several cases of typhoid fever. I want Dr Griffiths to come here immediately.'

'I'm sorry, but Dr Griffiths is out – on business.'

'When will he be back?' shouted Manson.

'I don't know.'

'But listen . . .'

But the speaker at the other end had gone. Manson swore loudly. Turning round he saw Annie, the servant, beside him.

'Dr Griffiths is never at home at this hour of the day,' she told him. 'He's out enjoying himself.'

'But I think that it was Dr Griffiths who spoke to me.'

Annie smiled, 'Perhaps. When he is at home, he pretends that he's out! I shouldn't waste your time on him!'

That evening, while attending to his surgery patients, Andrew decided to see Denny. 'It was he who suggested typhoid,' he reminded himself. 'I hate him, but that doesn't matter. I must go to him at once.'

Denny showed no surprise when Andrew visited him. 'Well! Have you killed anybody yet?' he asked in his rude manner.

Andrew reddened. 'You were right. It is typhoid. I've come to ask your advice.'

Denny gave a faint smile. 'Then you'd better come in. Sit down. Have a drink? No! I didn't think that you would!' For a few moments he sat in silence, pushing the dog Hawkins with his foot. Then he pointed to the table and said: 'Look at that.'

On the table stood a microscope. Andrew looked through this and saw, on a glass plate, the bacteria that were responsible for the fever.

'You have typhoid cases too, then?' Andrew asked with interest.

'Four – and all in the same area as yours. These bacteria come from the well in Glydar Place.'

Andrew looked at him in surprise.

'The sewer is the cause of the trouble,' Denny continued. 'There are holes in it; and the dirt flows through these into the well. I've reported the matter to Griffiths several times, but he refuses to do anything.'

'It's shameful!' Andrew almost shouted. He got up and moved towards the door. 'Thank you for the information. In future, I shall order all my patients in Glydar Place to boil their water.'

'It's Griffiths who ought to be boiled!' Denny laughed. 'We shall probably have to see more of each other before this situation improves. Come and see me any time that you can bear it.'

Going home by Glydar Place, where he left orders regarding the water, Andrew realized that he did not hate Denny as much as he thought. Denny's behaviour seemed strange to Andrew, and when he arrived home, he decided to look up his qualifications in one of Page's old medical books. He found that Denny, who came of a good family, had been educated at an English university, and had qualified with good degrees at one of the best hospitals in London.

Denny was, in fact, an excellent doctor. He gave his patients the best possible attention, and treated them with great kindness. But he refused to give medicines unless they were necessary. Many doctors did not trouble to find out what was really wrong with their patients, but just gave them useless medicines. This made Denny bitterly critical of medical practice, and accounted for his strange behaviour at times.

Chapter 3   The Sewer

Andrew worked hard to cure his fever cases. Now that his patients were drinking only boiled water, they quickly began to get better. 'I am succeeding!' he called out in delight.

Then, one day in November, just before lunch, Denny telephoned him.

'Manson, I'd like to see you. Can you come to my house at three o'clock? It's important.'

'Very well. I'll be there.'

Andrew ate his lunch in deep thought. As he ate, Miss Page looked at him suspiciously and asked: 'Who telephoned you? It was Denny, wasn't it? I told you not to see that man. He's worthless!'

Andrew replied angrily: 'You're wrong, Miss Page! I have found him extremely helpful.'

'He's a bad doctor. He refuses to give medicines. He's so rude, too! I forbid you to see him.'

They finished their meal in silence. After lunch, Andrew walked slowly up the street towards Denny's house.

Philip greeted him with the news: 'Young Jones died this morning. And I have two new typhoid cases.'

Andrew looked down at the floor in sympathy, hardly knowing what to say.

'Don't look so pleased about it,' Denny said bitterly. 'You like to see my cases get worse, while yours get better! But if that sewer–'

'No, no!' Andrew interrupted. 'I'm sorry – honestly, I am. We must do something about the sewer. We must write to–'

'It's no use writing letters!' Philip cried. 'There's only one way to make them build a new sewer.'

'What's that?'

'Blow up the old one!'

Andrew was not sure if Denny had gone mad. 'But you're not being serious.'

Denny looked at him with scorn. 'You needn't help me, if you don't want to.'

'Oh, I'll help you,' Andrew promised.

All that afternoon, while visiting his patients, Manson wished he hadn't made the promise. Denny's plan was too risky! If they were discovered, they would both be dismissed from their posts. Andrew trembled at this thought. He was angry with Philip; swore a number of times that he would not go. But, for some reason, he could not break his promise.

At 11 o'clock that night, Denny and he set out with the dog, Hawkins. It was very dark and wet, and a strong wind blew the rain into their faces. The two men, each of whom carried explosives in his coat pockets, walked quickly along the empty streets. When they reached the sewer in Glydar Place, they broke open the lid, which had not been lifted for many years, and then shone a light inside.

'Nice, isn't it?' said Denny. 'See the holes in the wall? Look, Manson – look for the last time!'

No more was said. They placed their explosives inside the sewer, put back the lid, and then ran up the street.

When they were only about 25 metres away, there was a loud explosion.

'We've done it, Denny!' Andrew said excitedly.

Five more explosions followed, the last so loud that it could be heard all down the valley.

'There!' said Denny. 'That's the end of that particular cause of misery!'

Almost immediately, doors and windows opened and people ran out of their houses. In a minute the street was crowded. Making good use of the darkness and the noise, Denny and Manson hurried home.

Before eight o'clock the next morning, Dr Griffiths arrived on the scene. He had been sent for by several of the most important men in the town, who told their Medical Officer in loud voices, so that everyone could hear, that he had neglected his duty most shamefully.

When they had finished with him, Griffiths walked over to Denny who, with Manson, stood in the crowd listening to the angry exchanges.

'Well, Denny,' he said, 'I'll have to build that new sewer for you now.'

Denny's face showed no expression. 'I warned you about this several months ago,' he said coldly. 'Don't you remember?'

'Yes, yes! But how could I guess that the thing would blow up? It's a mystery to me how it happened.'

The work of building a new sewer began on the following Monday.

Chapter 4   A Visit to the School

It was three months later, and Andrew was beginning to like the dirty old town and its strange, but kind, people.

Feeling extremely happy, he went out one afternoon to see a small boy of nine, whose name was Joe. He was not very ill, but as the family was poor his illness seemed likely to give the boy's mother a lot more work.

At the end of his visit, Andrew remarked to her: 'You must still keep his brother home from school, I'm afraid.'

Joe's mother looked at him in surprise. 'But Miss Barlow said that I needn't keep him at home.'

Although he was sympathetic, Andrew felt annoyed. 'Oh! And who is Miss Barlow?' he asked.

'She's the schoolteacher. She called to see me this morning.'

Andrew did not reply. But on leaving the house, he walked straight to the school to see this teacher. When he entered the classroom, all the children were sitting at their desks. Miss Barlow was facing away from him, and did not notice him at first. Then suddenly she turned round.

She was so different from most schoolteachers he had met that Andrew paused uncertainly.

'Are you Miss Barlow?' he asked awkwardly.

'Yes.' She was a small, attractive and well-dressed young woman of about twenty-two. She looked at him for a moment, and then smiled. 'You work for Dr Page, don't you?'

'Never mind about that!' he answered coldly. 'I am Dr Manson. You have a boy here whose brother has a serious disease that could spread to other children. He ought to be at home.'

She smiled again. 'Yes, I know.'

Her refusal to treat his visit seriously made Andrew lose his temper. 'Don't you realize that you are breaking the rules by allowing this boy to come to school?'

His manner now made Miss Barlow angry. But she replied quietly: 'Most of the children here have already had the same illness, and the others are certain to catch it in any case. And if he didn't come to school he would miss his free milk, which is doing him such a lot of good.'

'He ought to be at home! You must send that child home at once,' Andrew ordered her.

Her eyes showed her anger now. '*I* am in charge of this class. You may be able to tell people in other places what to do, but here I give the orders.'

'You're breaking the law!' he shouted. 'I shall have to report you.'

'Then report me,' Miss Barlow replied. She turned to the children and said: 'Stand up, children, and say: 'Good morning, Dr Manson. Thank you for coming.''

The children rose and politely repeated the words. She then showed him out of the door and gently closed it behind him.

Chapter 5   Christine

Manson wrote several letters, but he tore them all up again. He felt angry with himself because he had lost his temper. He decided not to report the schoolteacher. He tried to forget the matter, but he could not dismiss Christine Barlow from his mind.

13

Two weeks later, when he was walking down the street, Mrs Bramwell called out to him: 'Oh, Dr Manson! I want to see you. Will you come to dinner tonight? I've invited three other very nice people – Mr and Mrs Watkins from the mine, and the schoolteacher, Christine Barlow.'

Manson's face lit up with pleasure. 'Well – of course I'll come, Mrs Bramwell. Thank you for asking me.'

For the rest of the day, he could think of nothing but the fact that he was going to meet Christine Barlow again. After the evening surgery, he hurried round to the Bramwells' house. He felt very awkward. He did not dare even to look at Christine during dinner, and he did not address a single remark to her after the meal. He wanted to speak to her, but he did not have the courage to do so. But when the dinner party ended, he spoke to her as she was leaving the house.

'Miss Barlow, may I take you home?' he asked.

'Thank you, but Mr and Mrs Watkins have already offered to take me,' she told him.

Andrew felt very disappointed. 'I want to say that I'm sorry!' he said suddenly. 'I behaved very badly. Your decision about that boy was right. I admire you for it. Good night!'

He did not wait for her answer. He turned round and walked down the road. For the first time for many days, he felt happy.

Andrew had never been in love before. He was afraid to fall in love – afraid that it might get in the way of his work. But he could not control his feelings for Christine. He wanted with all his heart to see her again.

Then, one day in May, he received a note from her inviting him to supper.

On the following evening, he almost ran to the house where Christine lived. He arrived early – before the Watkins, who had also been invited.

Christine gave him a warm welcome. He was so pleased that

he could hardly speak.

'It's been a lovely day, hasn't it?' he said, as he followed her into the living room.

'Lovely,' she agreed. 'I went for such a nice walk this afternoon.'

She sat down. How nice it was to be here with her! Her room, full of her own possessions, was pleasant and comfortable. He felt relaxed, and began to ask her questions about herself.

She answered him simply. Her mother had died when she was fifteen; and, four years later, her father and brother had been killed in an accident in their coal mine. Now she had no relatives. 'People were kind to me,' she said. 'Mr and Mrs Watkins were especially kind. I came to work at the school here.' She paused. 'But I'm like you – I still feel strange, a little lonely, here.'

He looked at her. 'It's easy to feel lonely here. I often wish that I had somebody to talk to.'

She smiled. 'What do you want to talk about?'

He turned red. 'Oh, my work, I suppose. I seem to have so many problems,' he explained.

'Do you mean that you have difficult cases?'

'No – not really.' He paused. 'When I came to Drineffy, I imagined that a doctor's life would be very pleasant; but now I am discovering that it is far from that. The system is all wrong. For example, a patient comes to the surgery for a bottle of medicine and is given coloured water! It isn't right! Doctors don't take enough trouble to find out what is wrong with a patient before treating him. They are always in such a hurry!'

Christine was about to answer when the doorbell rang. She rose, saying: 'I hope that you will tell me more about this another time.'

Mr Watkins and his wife came in, and almost at once they sat down to supper. It was a good meal, and nicely served. After supper Mr Watkins told stories which made them all laugh. The evening passed quickly. When Andrew looked at his watch he saw, to his surprise, that it was nearly 11 o'clock.

Sadly, he rose to leave. He thanked Christine, who went with him to the door. 'Please can I see you again?' He paused. 'Will you – Christine, will you come out with me one evening?'

She smiled. 'Well – I might!'

He wanted to kiss her. He held her hand for a moment, turned, and ran down the path on his way home. Oh! She was a lovely girl! And he had called her Christine!

Chapter 6   Curing a "Madman"

Andrew felt happy, hopeful. This feeling of excitement influenced his work: he wanted to do something to make Christine proud of him.

For the next few weeks, he had only very simple cases to attend to, such as cuts on the hand and colds in the head. He began to ask himself if a doctor in such a lonely place would ever have an opportunity to do work of real importance.

But then, at six o'clock one morning, he was woken by Annie who, with tears in her eyes, gave him a note from Dr Bramwell. Andrew quickly opened the envelope and read: 'Come at once. I want you to help me with a dangerous madman.'

'It's my brother Emlyn, Doctor,' said Annie, wiping her eyes. 'He's been ill for three weeks. During the night he suddenly became violent and attacked his wife with a knife. Come quickly, Doctor.'

Andrew dressed in three minutes, and went with Annie to Emlyn's home. There he found Bramwell, seated at a table, writing.

'Ah, Manson! Thank you for coming so quickly!' he said.

'What's the matter?'

'Emlyn has gone mad. We shall have to send him to the mental hospital at once. But, of course, they will not admit him unless a second doctor signs my report, saying that he is mad. That's why I sent for you.'

'What are your reasons for considering him mad?' Andrew asked.

Bramwell read out his report.

'It certainly sounds bad,' Andrew agreed, when Bramwell had finished. 'Well, I'll examine him.'

Emlyn was in bed, and seated beside him – in case he should become violent again – were two of his friends from the mine. At the foot of the bed stood his wife, who was crying.

Andrew had a sudden feeling of coldness, almost of fear. He went over to Emlyn; and, at first, the man hardly recognised him. Andrew spoke to him. Emlyn gave a reply that did not make sense. Then, throwing up his hands, he shouted and threatened Andrew. A silence followed.

Emlyn showed all the signs of madness. But, for some reason, Andrew doubted whether he was really mad. He kept asking himself why Emlyn should behave like this. There might be some other medical reason. He touched the man's swollen face, and noticed with surprise that his finger left no mark. At once he saw the cause of the trouble. He finished his examination to make certain that he was right, and then went back to Bramwell.

'Listen, Bramwell,' he said, trying to hide his excitement, 'I don't think that we should sign that report.'

'What? But the man's mad!'

'That's not my opinion,' Andrew answered. 'In my opinion, Emlyn is only suffering from a hormone problem.'

Bramwell was too surprised to speak.

'Let us try to cure him, instead of sending him to the mental hospital,' Andrew suggested.

Before Bramwell could argue, Andrew went out of the room.

A few minutes later, he returned with Emlyn's wife and told her, with Bramwell listening, what they planned to do.

Two weeks after starting Andrew's new treatment, Emlyn was well enough to leave his sickbed; and in two months he was back at work.

One evening he and his wife went to the surgery and told Andrew: 'We owe everything to you. We would like you to be our regular doctor in future. Bramwell knows nothing: he's a silly old fool!'

'You can't change doctors,' Andrew answered. 'That would not be fair to Bramwell.'

But Andrew felt pleased that they wished to change; and, as soon as they left, he went round to Christine to tell her of his success.

Chapter 7   Freddie Hamson

In July an important meeting of British doctors was held in the Welsh capital, Cardiff. Andrew had not intended to go to this meeting, because of the cost, but a few days before it began he received a letter from his friend Freddie Hamson, urging him to attend and inviting him to have dinner with him on the Saturday evening.

Andrew showed the letter to Christine, with whom he was now very much in love, and asked her: 'Will you come with me? I'd like you to meet Hamson.'

'I'd love to come,' she said.

On Saturday Christine and Andrew took the train to Cardiff. Andrew smiled at Christine, who sat on the opposite seat. He wanted to kiss her, to hold her in his arms. Rather breathlessly, he said: 'We shall have a happy time this evening. Freddie's a nice man. You'll like him.'

When they reached Cardiff, they went to the hotel where the meeting was being held. Hamson had not yet arrived. So they stood together, watching the doctors and their wives talking and laughing.

After some time, Freddie arrived and headed towards them. 'Hullo! Hullo! Sorry I'm late. Well, well! It's nice to see you again, Andrew. I see that you're still the same old Manson! Why don't you buy yourself a new suit?' Suddenly noticing Christine, he smiled and ordered Andrew: 'Introduce me, man! Wake up!'

While the two doctors were in their meeting, Christine went out to look at the shops. Then, in the early evening, they met up again in the hotel. Over dinner Freddie began to talk about the days when he and Andrew had studied medicine together. 'I never thought then,' he said in a rather scornful manner, 'that you would bury yourself in the country like this!'

'Do you really think that he's buried himself?' Christine asked coldly.

There was a pause. Freddie smiled at Andrew. 'What did you think of the meeting?'

'I suppose,' Andrew answered doubtfully, 'that the discussions help to keep one's knowledge up to date.'

'Oh, I don't take any notice of the discussions. Heavens, no! I've come here to meet the doctors – the important doctors who will be useful to me in my profession. You'd be surprised how many useful men there are here. When I return to London, I shall invite them to a meal. Then we shall do business together.'

'I don't understand, Freddie,' Manson said.

'It's simple! When rich people come to me, I shall examine them first, and then send them to a second doctor to see if he agrees with my opinion about their illness and the treatment to give. In return, these doctors will send me some of their patients. The patients then have to pay each of us. That's the way to make money!' Freddie laughed. 'You ought to come to London one day. Then you and I could do business together!'

Christine looked quickly at Hamson, was about to speak, but then stopped herself.

'And now tell me about yourself, Manson,' Freddie continued, smiling. 'What have you been doing?'

'Oh, nothing much. Most of my patients are coal miners and their families.'

'That doesn't sound very good!'

'I enjoy my work,' Andrew said.

Christine interrupted. 'And you do important work.'

'Yes, I had one interesting case recently.' Andrew began to tell Hamson about Emlyn. But Hamson was not really listening.

At ten o'clock Andrew and Christine left. As they walked back to the railway station, Andrew asked: 'Did you like Hamson?'

'No − not much.' She paused. 'He's too pleased with himself. He considers himself to be so much better than you. I hate that way of talking.'

Andrew seemed surprised. 'I agree that he is rather pleased with himself, but he's really a very nice man.'

'You must be blind if you can't see the kind of person he is! He only thinks about himself!' Andrew had never seen Christine so angry before.

They entered the railway station. Andrew wanted a quiet talk with Christine to clear up their little disagreement, and to tell her of his love for her. But the train was crowded and they could not be alone.

It was late when they reached Drineffy, and Christine looked very tired. So he took her home and said good night.

Chapter 8   Baby Morgan

It was nearly midnight when Andrew reached the Pages' house. He found Joe Morgan waiting for him. Morgan and his wife had been married for 20 years, and now, to their great joy, they were expecting their first baby.

'Oh, Doctor, I am glad to see you!' said Joe. 'My wife – come quickly.'

Andrew ran into the house for his bag of instruments, and then hurried along to Morgan's home.

'I'll wait outside, Doctor. I'm too worried to come in,' Morgan said, when they arrived.

Inside, a narrow staircase led up to a small bedroom, which, though clean, had very little furniture and was lit by only an oil lamp. Here Mrs Morgan's mother and a fat nurse stood anxiously by the bed, watching Andrew's expression as he moved about the room.

Andrew smiled. 'Don't worry!' he comforted them.

He knew that this case would demand all his attention. As there was nothing that he could do for the moment, he sat down and waited, thinking of Christine.

At half past three he went over to the bed and saw that he could now begin his work. It was a long and difficult birth. Then, just as daylight was beginning, the child was born – lifeless.

As he looked at the baby's still, white body, Andrew turned cold. Quickly, he gave the child to the nurse and turned his attention to Mrs Morgan, who was also close to death. Working with great speed, he seized a bottle and gave her a medicine to make her heart stronger; he then made a feverish effort to save her by other means. After a few minutes, her heartbeat strengthened. Seeing that she was out of danger, Andrew turned round to the nurse and shouted: 'Where's the child?'

The nurse looked afraid: she had put the baby under the bed.

At once Andrew knelt down and pulled out the child. Still kneeling, he examined the boy, and decided that there was just a chance of bringing him to life. He jumped to his feet and ordered the nurse: 'Get me some hot water – and cold water. Bowls, too! Quickly!'

'But, Doctor–'

'Quick!' he shouted.

When the bowls arrived, Andrew filled one with the cold water and the other with the hot water. Working with great speed, he then placed the baby first into one bowl and then into the other. He continued this operation for 15 minutes, but the baby showed no sign of life.

'You're wasting your time, Doctor,' said the nurse. 'It's dead!'

But Andrew took no notice. He put the baby into hot and cold water for another 15 minutes. Having again achieved no success, he then made a last and more determined effort, pressing on the baby's little chest, trying to get breath into its still body.

Suddenly, the baby made a movement. Gradually its white face and body began to turn pink. After a few more minutes, it started to cry.

'Good heavens!' the nurse cried. 'It's – it's come to life!'

Andrew handed her the child. He felt weak, almost faint. His dirty instruments, cloths and bowls lay in pools of water on the floor. Mrs Morgan was asleep, not knowing what had been happening. Her mother stood by the wall, praying.

'I'll come back for my bag later, Nurse,' Andrew said.

He went downstairs to the kitchen and put on his hat and coat.

Outside, he found Joe. 'All right, Joe,' he said. 'Your wife and son are both safe.'

It was nearly five o'clock. A few miners were already in the streets. As Andrew walked home, he thought: 'I've done something! Oh, God, I've done something good at last.'

Andrew had a bath and went downstairs to breakfast. Miss Page, having discovered that his bed had not been slept in, gave him a severe look as he sat down at the table, and remarked: 'You got home late! I suppose you were out enjoying yourself all night — drinking or getting into some other kind of trouble. You're as bad as all the other men we've employed — you can't be trusted!'

Andrew was too angry to reply. After the morning surgery, he went back to the Morgans. As he walked down their road, women whom he had never met smiled at him in a most friendly manner. When he reached the Morgans' house, he received a very warm welcome.

He went upstairs to the bedroom. The little room, which had been so untidy only a few hours before, had been cleaned and polished; and his instruments carefully washed and put into his bag. There were clean sheets on the bed.

The nurse rose from her seat and, smiling at the mother and baby, said: 'They look very well now, don't they, Doctor? But they don't know how much trouble they gave us!'

Mrs Morgan tried to express her thanks. 'We are very grateful to you, Doctor. Has Joe been to see you yet?' she asked. 'No? Well, he's coming.'

Before Andrew left the house, the old woman gave him a glass of wine.

Two weeks later, when Andrew had paid his last visit of the day, Morgan, who was about to go abroad with his wife and child, called to see him.

'Money can't pay for all that you have done for us, but my wife and I would like to give you this little present,' he said, handing Andrew a cheque for five pounds.

'But I can't accept this, Joe!' Andrew said. He knew that the Morgans had very little money.

'You must accept it. We want you to,' Joe told him. 'It's a

present for *yourself* – not for Dr Page. You understand?'

'Yes, I understand, Joe,' Andrew said, smiling.

He took the cheque to the Pages' bank and told the manager, Mr Rees, that he wished to open an account.

Rees looked at the cheque and asked slowly: 'Do you want this account to be in your own name?'

Manson was surprised at the question. 'Yes. Why? Is the amount too small?'

'Oh, no, Doctor. We're very pleased to do business with you. Er – you did say that you want the account to be in your own name?'

'Yes – of course.'

'All right, Doctor. I just wanted to check. Good morning, Dr Manson. Good morning!'

Manson left the bank, asking himself what the manager meant. It was some days before he was able to answer the question.

Chapter 9   Joe Morgan's Cheque

Christine had gone away for a holiday, and Andrew felt lonely without her. The weather was hot and tiring, and life seemed dull. Then one day Watkins sent a message, asking him to call at his office.

The manager of the coal mines greeted him in a friendly manner. 'Listen, Doctor,' he said. 'Emlyn and a number of the miners want me to hire you as one of the Company's doctors.'

Andrew looked at him in surprise. 'You mean–'

'I mean,' Watkins said slowly, 'that I would like to add your name to the list of doctors, so that any man who wishes to can leave Dr Page and make you his regular doctor.'

'I couldn't agree to that! It wouldn't be fair to Dr Page,' Andrew replied. 'It wouldn't be honest!'

Watkins was disappointed. 'Think about my suggestion, Doctor,' he urged Andrew.

'It's no use – I couldn't do it!' he said firmly, though sadly.

Wishing that he had never been offered this opportunity to improve his position, Andrew tried to take his mind off the matter by going to see Denny. But, to his disappointment, he found that Denny had been drinking and could neither behave nor talk sensibly. Andrew put him to bed and left.

The next morning, after surgery, he went back to Denny's house to see how he was. He found him in an even worse condition. Swearing about Denny and the summer heat, Andrew hurried out to visit Philip's patients as well as his own.

When he called on him in the evening, Denny shouted: 'The medical profession! Huh! It's the worst system in the world! It's not honest! Give me another drink.' He paused. 'Manson, you're a good man! I love you better than a brother. You and I should work together. We'd soon change the whole of this profession.'

Denny nearly fell over, and Andrew put him to bed for the second time. For the rest of that week, he did all Denny's work. Then, on Sunday, Denny was quite well again.

'I understand that you've been doing my work for me, Manson,' he said in a cold voice.

His manner was so cold that Andrew left the house at once in anger. 'He behaves as if he has generously allowed me to do his work!' Andrew said to himself. But his anger soon left him. He was fond of Philip, and respected his honesty and skill as a doctor.

When Andrew reached home, Miss Page shouted at him: 'Is that you, Doctor? Dr Manson! I want you!'

'What's the matter, Miss Page?' he answered with annoyance.

She came up to him. 'What, you may well ask! Kindly explain this!' she said, holding up Joe Morgan's cheque.

Raising his head, Andrew saw Rees standing behind Miss Page.

'Yes, you have reason to be surprised!' Miss Page continued. 'Perhaps you will explain why you paid this money into your bank account instead of into Dr Page's.'

Andrew felt hot with anger. 'It's my money! Joe Morgan gave it to me as a present.'

'A present! It's easy to say that, now that he's abroad!'

'Write and ask him, if you doubt my word.'

'I do doubt your word! You are trying to take over Dr Page's practice. This shows the kind of man that you are. You consider only your own interests.'

Andrew moved towards them, his eyes on Rees. 'Miss Page,' he said, 'unless you take those words back within two minutes, I shall bring an action against you in a court of law – and I shall punish your bank manager in a way that he has never been punished before!'

'I – I only did my duty,' the bank manager said weakly.

'I'm waiting, Miss Page,' Andrew warned her.

She realized that she had said too much. 'I – I'm sorry.'

Andrew took a quick, deep breath. 'Miss Page, there is something that I want to tell you. Last week I was invited to become an official doctor to the Mining Company, but I refused the offer because I did not consider it fair to Dr Page to accept. Now I'm so tired of you that I have decided to leave. I give you a month's notice.'

She looked at him in surprise. 'Lies – all lies!' she shouted. 'You can't give me notice!'

Andrew said nothing more. He went upstairs to his room and closed the door.

Chapter 10   A New Post

Andrew began to search at once for another position. But he did not receive a single answer to his letters. He became very worried. How was he to live?

Then one day, when walking sadly down the street, he met Denny.

Knocking out the ashes from his pipe, Philip said: 'I'm sorry that you're leaving, Manson.' He paused. 'I heard this afternoon that the Aberalaw Medical Society is advertising for a new man. Aberalaw – that's 50 kilometres down the valley. Why don't you try for the post?'

Andrew looked doubtful. 'Well, yes,' he agreed slowly, 'I could try.'

He walked home, and wrote to the Society.

A week later, Andrew and seven other young doctors went to Aberalaw to be examined by the Society's committee. It was a fine summer afternoon and Andrew liked Aberalaw, which was larger than Drineffy with good streets and shops, and green fields surrounding the town. 'But I won't get this post,' he told himself, as he waited his turn for examination. The other men were better dressed and seemed more confident than he. But what would Christine think of him if he failed? She would return to Drineffy either today or tomorrow. He had not told her about the post; he wanted to surprise her, and to win her respect, by greeting her with the good news that he had been given the post.

Andrew, the third man to be examined, entered the committee room with a feeling of fear and determination. About 30 miners were in the room. At a small table sat a pale man with a kind face. He was Owen, the secretary.

Owen, in a quiet voice, explained the medical system at Aberalaw. 'The miners pay part of their wages each week to the

Society; and, out of this money, the Society provides the medical services, including a hospital. The Society employs a head doctor, Dr Llewellyn, four other doctors to help him, and a dentist; each doctor receives a payment for every patient on his list.' Owen turned to the committee. 'And now, gentlemen, do you wish to ask Dr Manson any questions?'

Several voices began to shout questions at Andrew. He answered them calmly, and returned to the waiting room. The next man then went in.

The last man came back from his examination with a smile of satisfaction on his face. 'I'm the winner!' his expression seemed to say.

There was another long wait. At last, the door of the committee room opened and Owen came out. He called out: 'Will you come in for a minute, Dr Manson? The committee would like to see you again.'

His heart beating fast, Andrew followed the secretary back into the committee room, where he was welcomed by smiling faces.

Owen now addressed him: 'Dr Manson, we will be honest with you. The committee, on Dr Llewellyn's advice, had intended to hire a doctor with experience in this valley; but the committee now feels that you may be a better choice.'

Andrew was too excited to smile.

'I should add, Dr Manson,' Owen continued, 'that the committee has been influenced by two letters, received from doctors in your own town. One is from a Dr Denny, who has a very good degree, and the other, enclosed with Denny's, is signed by Dr Page, by whom you are employed. These two doctors praise your work so highly that the committee would like to offer you the post.'

Andrew lowered his eyes, his thoughts on Denny's generous act.

'There is just one difficulty, Dr Manson,' Owen added. 'This post should really be given to a married man. The miners like their families to be attended by married doctors. Also, a house is provided.'

There was a long silence. They were all looking at him. At last, Andrew said calmly: 'That is all right, gentlemen. I am going to marry a girl in Drineffy.'

There were loud cheers.

'Then, Dr Manson, you are appointed,' said Owen. 'When can you start your duties?'

'I can start work next week,' Andrew answered. Then he turned cold as he thought: 'Suppose that Christine won't marry me!'

A few minutes later, Andrew left and excitedly ran to the railway station to catch the next train home to Drineffy.

When he reached Drineffy, he went straight to Christine's house to see if she had returned from her holiday. Finding, to his joy, that the light was on in her room, he rushed into the house.

'Christine!'

She looked at him in surprise. 'Andrew! How nice of you to come round!'

'Chris, I have something to tell you!'

A worried expression spread across her face. 'What has happened? Have you had more trouble with Miss Page? Are you going away?'

He shook his head. 'Christine! I've got a new post – an excellent post! At Aberalaw. Five hundred pounds a year and a house. A house, Christine! Oh, my dearest – Christine – could you – will you marry me?'

She went very pale. Her eyes were bright. She said quietly: 'And I thought that you were going to tell me some bad news!'

'No, no – the best news, my dear,' he cried. 'Oh Chris, I love you so much, but – perhaps you don't love me.'

She went towards him and laid her head against his chest. As he put his arm round her, she said: 'Oh, Andrew dear, I've loved you ever since – ever since I saw you walk into my school.'

Chapter 11   The Move to Aberalaw

A few days later they were married. On the same morning, they packed Christine's few pieces of furniture and pots and pans into John Lossin's old motor bus and drove slowly through the mountains to Aberalaw.

The weather was bright and sunny. They laughed and joked; and Lossin, a man without cares, kept pulling a bottle from his pocket to drink to their future happiness. They had lunch at a small hotel high in the mountains. Then they began to drop down into the valley leading to Aberalaw, along a rough and narrow road with steep hills on either side.

At last, after passing two dangerous bends, they caught their first sight of Aberalaw. It was a moment of joy. The town lay before them, with its houses dotted up and down the valley; its shops, offices and churches were at one end of the town and, at the other end, its mines and smoking chimneys – all lit up by the bright sun.

'Look Chris – look!' Andrew whispered, pressing her arm tightly. 'It's a fine place, isn't it? There's the square! And look – there's the gas works. No need to use oil lamps here, dear. Where do you think our house is?'

They stopped a miner, who directed them to Vale View.

'Well!' said Christine as they entered the large, ugly house, Vale View, that was now their home. 'It's – it's nice, isn't it?'

'Yes, dear. It – it looks a lovely house.'

Excitedly, they went into each room. There were so many rooms, and they were all so large, that they only had enough furniture for two of them. They finished their tour of the house in the kitchen, where Christine unpacked some eggs and cooked a meal.

'Heavens, dear, you are a good cook! That was the best meal that I've ever eaten!' Andrew said in delight. 'Oh, I am looking forward to starting work! There ought to be good opportunities here – big opportunities!' He suddenly caught sight of a box in the corner. 'I say, Chris, what's that?'

'A wedding present – from Denny.'

'Denny!' His expression changed. Philip's manner had been cold when Andrew thanked him for his help in getting the new post, and told him of his intention to marry Christine. This morning, he had not even said goodbye to them. His unfriendly behaviour had hurt Andrew. Andrew slowly opened the box, thinking that it might be a joke. Then he gave a cry of delight. Inside was Denny's microscope and a note: 'I don't really need this. Good luck!'

Andrew picked up the microscope, carried it into another room, and gently laid it on the floor, saying: 'Owing to the generosity of our good friend Philip Denny, I shall now make this room my work room.'

Suddenly the telephone rang.

'Perhaps it's a patient, Chris! My first Aberalaw case!' Andrew cried, and ran into the hall to answer the telephone. It was Dr Llewellyn.

'Hullo, Manson. How are you? I want to welcome you and your wife to Aberalaw.'

'Thank you, Dr Llewellyn. That's most kind of you,' Andrew replied.

'Nonsense! Nonsense! Come and have dinner with us tonight. Then you and I can have a talk. We shall expect you at seven o'clock. Goodbye.'

Andrew hurried back to Christine to tell her about the invitation. 'Wasn't that nice of him, Chris? *The head doctor!* And he sounded so friendly! Mrs Manson, we are going to be successful!' He put his arm round her and began to dance.

Dr and Mrs Llewellyn greeted them like old friends. During dinner, while Mrs Llewellyn was talking to Christine, Dr Llewellyn told Andrew a few more details about the medical system at Aberalaw.

'There are two surgeries – one at the west end of the town and the other at the east end.' he explained. 'You will work at the west surgery with old Dr Urquhart and Gadge, who mixes the medicines. Here, at the east surgery, there are two other doctors: Dr Medley and Dr Oxborrow. They're all nice men. You'll like them. Of course, I'm too busy to work at the surgery myself. I have so many other responsibilities! I'm in charge of the hospital. I'm Medical Officer for the town, and hold several other important posts. I also have a private practice.'

'You *do* have a lot of work!' Manson remarked.

Llewellyn smiled. 'I must make money, Dr Manson!' He paused. 'I should just mention that the doctors have agreed to pay me a small part of their salaries.'

Andrew looked up in surprise.

'That's because I see their patients for them when they're worried,' Llewellyn added quickly. 'But we'll discuss this matter at another time.'

At that moment, Mrs Llewellyn called to her husband from the other end of the table: 'They were only married this morning! Mrs Manson has just told me so.' She took Christine's hand. 'My poor child! You will be busy – trying to make that terrible house look nice.'

Manson reddened. 'It's true,' he admitted. He paused. 'Would it be possible, do you think, Dr Llewellyn, for me to go to London for two days to buy furniture for our house?'

'Certainly! You can be absent from work tomorrow and the next day, Dr Manson.'

At ten o'clock Llewellyn drove Andrew and Christine to the hospital, where he had some patients to see. The hospital, though small, was well built and seemed to contain everything that was needed. As Llewellyn showed them round, Andrew thought: 'This is perfect! I'll be able to treat my patients very effectively in here!'

'I'm rather proud of this place, Manson,' Llewellyn remarked.

Then suddenly his manner changed. 'Well, I can't waste any more time,' he said quickly. 'You can find your way home, can't you? Good night!'

As they walked home together, Andrew said: 'I like him. I like him very much. But – but why should we pay him part of our salary? It doesn't seem fair!'

When they returned to their almost empty house, they stood together in the dark hall. Then Andrew put his arm round Christine and whispered: 'What's your name, love?'

'Christine,' she answered in surprise.

'Christine what?'

'Christine Manson.' Her breath came quickly, and was warm on his lips.

Chapter 12   The System at Aberalaw

They went to London and bought some cheap furniture, arranging to pay for this at the rate of a few pounds a month during the next year.

On Thursday morning Andrew began work at the west surgery. His first patient was a man with a bad knee, who wanted a doctor's note stating that he was not fit for work. Andrew examined his knee and gave him his note. But the next three patients also asked for doctor's notes.

Andrew got up, opened the door of the waiting room, and

called out: 'How many more men want sick notes? Stand up, please.'

Forty men were waiting and they all stood up.

It was half past ten when Andrew finished his surgery. Then an old man with a red face walked into his room. This was Dr Urquhart.

'Heavens, man!' said Urquhart, without a word of introduction. 'Where have you been during these last two days? I had to do your work for you. Never mind! Never mind! I'll say no more about it. Come and meet Gadge. He's a miserable man, but he's good at his work.'

Andrew followed Urquhart into another room, where Gadge, a thin man with a sad expression, took hardly any notice of him.

'Well,' said Urquhart, after introducing them, 'is there anything that you would like to know?'

'I'm worried about the number of sick notes that I had to sign this morning.' Andrew told him. 'Some of the men seemed quite fit for work. A doctor shouldn't give sick notes for no reason.'

Urquhart looked at him quickly. 'Take care! The men will be annoyed if you refuse them their sick notes.'

For the only time that morning, Gadge made a remark: 'That's because there's nothing wrong with most of them!'

All that day, Andrew worried about the sick notes. He decided to give no more unless they were really necessary. He went to his evening surgery with an anxious but determined expression.

The crowd was larger than at the morning surgery. The first patient to enter was a big, fat man who looked as if he had never done an honest day's work in his life. His name was Ben Chenkin.

'Sick note!' he said roughly.

'What for?' Andrew asked.

Chenkin held out his hand. 'Skin disease. Look!'

34

Andrew could see at once that there was nothing seriously wrong with Chenkin. He rose from his seat. 'Take off your clothes,' he ordered him.

Chenkin now asked: 'What for?'

'I'm going to examine you.'

Chenkin, who had never been examined by the last doctor, undressed.

Andrew carried out a long examination. Then he said sharply: 'Dress again, Chenkin.' He sat down and began to write out a note.

'I thought that you'd give me one,' Chenkin said rudely.

He seized the note from Andrew's hand, and rushed out of the surgery. Five minutes later, he returned.

'What's the meaning of this?' he shouted, pushing the paper into Andrew's face.

It read: 'This is to state that Chenkin is suffering from the effects of drinking too much, but is quite fit to work.'

'I've got skin disease!' shouted Chenkin. 'I've had it for 15 years!'

'Well, you haven't got it now,' Andrew said. A crowd had collected by the open door. He could see Urquhart looking anxious and Gadge with a faint smile on his face.

'Are you going to give me a sick note?' Chenkin shouted.

'No, I'm not,' Andrew shouted back. 'And get out of here before I throw you out.'

Chenkin looked as if he might kill Andrew. Then he turned and, shouting threats, left the surgery.

As soon as he had gone, Gadge entered, rubbing his hands with delight. 'Do you know who he is? His son is an important member of the committee.'

The Chenkin event caused a lot of talk. Some people were pleased that Chenkin had been made to work at last. But most people were on his side.

As he went round the town, calling on his patients, Andrew received many black looks. And there was worse trouble for him. The men had the right to choose their doctor. Each man gave his medical card to the doctor of his choice; if he wished to make a change, he could ask for his card back and hand it to another doctor. Every night that week men came to Andrew's surgery and demanded, 'My card, please, Doctor.'

Every card that he returned reduced his salary.

Urquhart warned him: 'Take care, man! I understand how you feel – you want to improve matters. But take care! Think before you act.'

Andrew soon ran into more trouble. He was called to the home of Thomas Evans, a miner who had burnt his left arm. When Andrew arrived, he found that the Area Nurse, who had since left the house, had put oil on the burn.

Andrew examined the arm and saw that unless he changed the treatment at once, the arm would become infected. So, with great care, he cleaned and treated the burn and put on a new bandage.

'Will it be all right, Doctor?' Evans asked anxiously, when he had finished.

'Yes – quite all right.' Andrew smiled. 'Leave this to Nurse and me!'

Before he left the house, he wrote a short note to the nurse, thanking her for what she had done, and asking her to continue his treatment.

Next morning, when he went back to the house, he found that his bandage had been removed, and that the arm had again been treated with oil.

The nurse was waiting for him. 'What's the explanation of this?' she asked angrily.

Andrew felt annoyed, but he managed to smile. 'Now, Nurse, don't–'

'I've worked here for 20 years; and nobody has ever told me

before not to use oil on a burn!'

'Now, listen, Nurse,' Andrew tried to reason. 'There's a danger of infection. That's why I want you to try my treatment.'

'I've never heard of this treatment! Old Dr Urquhart doesn't give it. I refuse to take orders from a man who has been here for only a week!'

It was dangerous to quarrel with the nurse. But Andrew could not risk his patient's health. He said in a low voice: 'If *you* won't give my treatment, Nurse, I shall come in every morning and evening and give it myself.'

'All right – do!' the nurse shouted. 'And I hope that Evans lives through it.'

She then rushed out of the house.

In silence, Andrew attended to the damaged arm. When he left, he promised to return at nine o'clock that night.

But that same evening, Mrs Evans went to his surgery and, in a frightened voice, said: 'I'm sorry to trouble you, Doctor, but can I have my husband's card back, please?'

Andrew rose without a word, searched for the card, and handed it to her.

When he returned home after surgery, he was very silent. After supper, he sat down beside Christine and, leaning his head against her, said sadly: 'Oh, my dear, I've begun so badly!' Tears came to his eyes.

Chapter 13   The Vaughans

Andrew had a very difficult time. All Chenkin's friends and relatives were his enemies, and the Area Nurse tried to persuade his patients to leave him.

He had another bitter disappointment: Dr Llewellyn refused to let him use the hospital.

'What do you think happened this morning, Chris?' Andrew said to his wife with disgust. 'I wanted to give a man treatment in hospital – my first hospital case – and so I telephoned Llewellyn and asked his permission. Well, Llewellyn drove round in his expensive car to examine the man personally. He was very pleasant. He agreed at once to admit the patient into hospital. But then, before I could thank him, he told me that he would take over the case. He said that he attends to all the hospital patients and that – oh, what does it matter what he said?'

Andrew was beginning to consider himself a failure. But at the end of that week he received a visitor. Late one evening, the doorbell rang. It was Owen, the secretary to the Society.

Andrew turned white. Did the committee intend to dismiss him for his failure? Were he and Christine to be thrown out into the street? Then suddenly Owen produced a yellow card.

'I'm sorry to call so late, Dr Manson,' he said, 'but I want to give you my medical card. I would like you to be my doctor.'

Andrew could hardly speak. 'Thank you, Mr Owen. I'll – I'll be delighted to add your name to my list.'

Christine, who was standing in the hall, invited Owen into the living room, where they sat and talked.

'Don't lose heart!' Owen comforted Andrew. 'The people here are not easy to understand, but they are really very kind. When they know you better, they will like you and their manner towards you will change.'

Before Andrew could reply, Owen asked: 'Have you heard about Evans? No? That oil, which you warned the nurse not to use, did exactly what you were afraid would happen. He's lost the use of his arm, and will never be able to work again.'

Andrew expressed his sorrow. He felt very sad that a wound which could have got better so easily had ruined Evans's life.

After a short silence, Owen told them that he saw his purpose in life to make life happier for the miners of Aberalaw. He wanted to improve the medical services, to build better houses, and to make the mines themselves healthier and safer.

At this stage, Andrew told Owen that he believed that the dust from a certain kind of coal caused lung disease. 'These men work in the coal dust all day,' he said. 'They breathe it into their lungs. I may be wrong in my opinion, but I don't think so. What excites me is that nobody seems to have thought of this before!' he added eagerly.

Owen leaned forward. 'My goodness, Doctor, this is really important.'

They had a long discussion. It was late when the secretary left. As the front door closed behind Owen, Andrew thought: 'That man is my friend.'

The news that the secretary had given his card to Andrew spread quickly, and helped to make the new doctor a little more popular.

One afternoon in December, Andrew was returning home. He saw, coming towards him, a young man whom he recognized as Richard Vaughan, a director of the Aberalaw Mining Company. He tried to avoid him; but, to his surprise, Vaughan called out in a friendly voice: 'Hullo! You're the man who sent Chenkin back to work, aren't you?'

Andrew stopped.

'I would like to have seen old Chenkin's face!' Vaughan laughed.

'It didn't amuse me.'

Taking no notice of this remark, Vaughan said: 'You're our nearest neighbours. My wife will pay yours a visit now that you have settled in.'

'Thanks!' Andrew said coldly, and walked away.

When he reached home, he told Christine about their meeting. 'Why was he so friendly? It's a mystery to me!' he said. 'I've seen him pass Llewellyn in the street without even looking at him. Perhaps he hopes to persuade me to send more men back to work at his mines!'

'Oh, Andrew, don't be so stupid!' said Christine. 'That's your great fault: you're so suspicious of people.'

'I am suspicious of Vaughan. He's proud, and he has too much money! He's not sincere. His wife won't come to see us!'

But Mrs Vaughan did call on Christine – and Christine enjoyed her visit. Ten days later, Mrs Vaughan telephoned and invited them both to dinner.

Andrew answered the telephone himself. 'I'm sorry,' he said. 'I'm afraid that we can't come. I work at the surgery till nine o'clock every evening.'

'But not on Sunday!' Her voice was warm and pleasant. 'We shall expect you to dinner next Sunday. Goodbye.'

Andrew ran back to Christine. 'These rich friends of yours have invited us to dinner. We can't go!'

'Now listen to me, Andrew Manson!' Christine said firmly. 'You must not be so foolish. We're poor, and everybody knows that we are. But that doesn't matter! The Vaughans are rich, but they're kind and clever people. Why shouldn't we be friendly with them? Don't be ashamed of being poor.'

They went to the Vaughans on Sunday, and they received a warm welcome. There were two other guests, Mr and Mrs Challis.

Andrew, who had never been in such a grand house before, felt awkward. At dinner – a simple but good meal – he sat next to Mrs Vaughan, who tried to start a conversation by asking him how he considered that the medical services in Aberalaw might be improved.

'Well, I don't know . . .' he said, as soup ran from his spoon on to the tablecloth. 'I suppose . . .'

He could not discuss even his favourite subject. He looked down at his plate until, to his relief, Mrs Vaughan turned to talk to Challis, who had an important post at Cardiff University.

Christine was quite relaxed. Andrew saw her smiling at Challis; heard her take part in a most informed discussion. It surprised him to hear how well she argued with Challis. Several times she tried to bring Andrew into their discussion.

'My husband is very interested in the coal miners, Mr Challis. He's doing some experiments – on the breathing of coal dust.'

'Oh, yes?' said Challis, looking with interest towards Manson.

'Isn't that so, dear?' Christine encouraged him.

'Oh, I don't know,' Andrew answered. 'It's of no importance!'

He was angry with himself. Perhaps this man Challis might have helped him!

For some strange reason, he began to direct his anger towards Christine. As they walked home at the end of the evening, he was silent.

Christine remarked happily: 'We did have a nice time, didn't we, love?'

'Oh, a very nice time!' Andrew said bitterly.

Next day, his manner was the same. Then, in the evening, Mrs Vaughan sent Christine some books and flowers – and this kind act led to a quarrel.

'Look, love!' Christine cried. 'Isn't Mrs Vaughan kind?'

Andrew stiffened. 'Very kind! Books and flowers from the rich lady! I suppose that you need these things to help you to live with me! I'm too dull for you! I'm not one of those clever people that you met last night! I'm just a doctor!'

'Andrew!'

'It's true, isn't it? I could see by your behaviour at dinner last night. You're tired of me already!'

'How can you say such a thing?'

Andrew ran from the room, closing the door noisily behind him. For five minutes, he walked up and down the kitchen. Then

41

suddenly he ran back to Christine and took her into his arms.

'Chris, my dear!' he cried. 'I'm sorry. Forgive me. I'm just a jealous fool! I love you with all my heart.'

They held each other tightly.

Chapter 14   Fighting the System

Winter ended. Andrew now had the additional interest of his research into coal dust, which he had begun by medically examining every miner on his list. Christine helped by writing notes for him. Her knowledge continued to surprise him.

As the hours of daylight grew longer, Christine, without telling Andrew, began to make a garden, with the help of an old miner. One day, when crossing the broken bridge, Andrew discovered them at work by the stream.

'Hey, what are you doing?' he shouted from the bridge.

'Wait and see!' Christine called back.

She made a neat little garden in a corner of the rough ground; and a few weeks later she proudly led Andrew by the arm and showed him her first flower.

On the last Sunday in March, without warning, Denny paid them a visit. They were delighted to see him.

'Page is dead,' Philip said, as they sat down to lunch. 'Yes, the poor man died a month ago. Miss Page is going to marry your friend Rees, the bank manager!'

There was a pause while they thought of Edward Page.

'And how are you, Philip?' Andrew asked, at last.

'Oh, I don't know! I don't feel very content.' Denny smiled. 'Drineffy seems a lonely place since you people left. I think I shall go abroad for a time – if I can find myself a post!'

Andrew was silent, sad at the thought of this clever doctor wasting his life in this way.

They talked all afternoon, and Philip caught the last train back to Drineffy. When he had gone, Andrew realized how much he missed Philip's friendship. They had shared the same ideas about the medical profession, and had worked with the same aim.

But the other doctors at Aberalaw seemed to have no aims at all. Urquhart, though a kind man, was old and had lost interest in his work. Medley had such a serious hearing problem that, when his patients told him about their illnesses, he never heard a word; and so, rather than risk giving them the wrong treatment, he always gave them a bottle of some harmless medicine. Oxborrow was a bad doctor for whom there was no excuse: he had so little confidence in himself that, before treating the simplest case, he would kneel by the patient's bed and pray – and in the end he usually made him worse and had to send for Llewellyn! There was no friendship between the doctors: they did not like each other at all.

Andrew wanted to improve relations – to start a new system where the doctors would work together in a friendly spirit. He also wanted to stop the unfair arrangement of paying part of their salaries to Llewellyn.

He had made so many mistakes already that he did not dare to attempt this for the moment. But then, a week or two later, he met Con Boland.

Andrew had discovered a hole in his tooth and went to see the Society's dentist. As he walked up the path to Boland's house, he heard a loud hammering and saw, through the open door of a wooden building, a large man mending a car with a hammer. At the same moment, the man noticed him.

'Hullo!' he called out.

'Hullo!' Andrew answered.

'What do you want?'

'I want to make an appointment with the dentist. I'm Dr Manson.'

'I'm the dentist!' Boland laughed. 'I've been doing some work on my old car.' He put on his coat. 'Come with me to the surgery, and I'll deal with your tooth.'

At the surgery, which was almost as dirty as the garage, Con filled the hole, talking all the time. He had not washed his hands. He was a careless, pleasant man, who enjoyed life.

After filling the tooth, he threw his instruments into a bowl of water and invited Andrew to tea.

'I'd like you to meet my family,' he said.

Boland's wife and five children, the oldest of whom was called Mary, were already having their tea when Con and Andrew entered the living room. This room was also untidy; the children's toys were scattered all over the floor.

After they had been introduced, Mrs Boland said: 'I meant to call on Mrs Manson, Doctor. But I've been so busy.'

Con burst into loud laughter. 'Busy! She hadn't a good enough dress to wear – that's what she means!' He turned to Andrew. 'We are poor, Manson. We earn very little money, and of course we have to give some of it to the Big Chief!'

'Who? Who's the Big Chief?' Andrew asked.

'Llewellyn, of course! He takes money from me as well as from you!'

'But why? You're a dentist – not a doctor!'

'Oh, he examines a patient for me occasionally.'

'Listen, Boland,' Andrew said quickly. 'This arrangement is not fair! Why don't we refuse to pay?'

'Eh?'

'Let's get together and break off this agreement with Llewellyn,' Andrew suggested. 'We can ask the other doctors to join in with us too.'

Con gave Andrew his hand. 'Manson, I'll support you. We'll work together.'

Andrew raced home to Christine.

'Chris! Chris! I've met such a nice man – a dentist. Listen, dear, we're going to do battle with Llewellyn!' He laughed excitedly.

The following day Andrew discussed his plan with Owen, who was sympathetic. He then persuaded Urquhart, Oxborrow and Medley to come to his house that evening. Having made his arrangements, Andrew suddenly decided to warn Llewellyn. He spoke to Llewellyn at the hospital. 'Look here, Dr Llewellyn,' he said, 'it's only fair to tell you that we doctors object to paying you part of our salaries. I intend to suggest that we stop these payments. We're going to meet at my house tonight to discuss the matter.'

Before Llewellyn could reply, Andrew turned and left the room.

The meeting began at nine o'clock.

'Gentlemen!' said Andrew. 'Our system here is all wrong. We are all members of the same Medical Society; but, instead of helping each other, we are always quarrelling. The result is that we give ourselves additional work and we are not making the most of our skills. There's no organization in our profession! We should change our system – work out some plan that will help us all.' He paused to watch their faces. 'And we should also refuse to pay money to Llewellyn. It isn't fair! I spoke to Owen about it. He says that this is not a rule of the committee but a private arrangement between Llewellyn and ourselves.'

'That's correct,' Urquhart agreed. 'The arrangement was made nine years ago. Two doctors at the east surgery kept asking Llewellyn to examine their patients. So one day he called us all together and said that he refused to see any more of our cases unless we agreed to pay him part of our salaries. That's how it started.'

'But it's Llewellyn's duty, as head doctor, to examine our patients when we need his advice. His own salary is meant to

cover work of this nature. Why should we pay him as well?'
Andrew asked angrily.

'I agree! I agree!' said Con.

Oxborrow now spoke. 'Remember this: Dr Llewellyn is always
prepared to take over our difficult cases.'

Andrew looked at him with scorn. 'Do you *want* him to take
over your difficult cases?'

'Of course,' said Oxborrow. 'Who doesn't?'

'I don't,' Andrew shouted. 'I want to cure them myself. I–'

'Oxborrow's right,' Medley interrupted. 'The most important
thing in medical practice, Manson, is to get rid of one's difficult
cases.'

'What a suggestion!' Andrew said angrily.

The discussion continued for nearly an hour.

Andrew then repeated: 'We must refuse to pay. Llewellyn
knows that we intend to refuse. I told him so this afternoon.'

'What!' shouted the three doctors. 'You told Llewellyn!'

'Of course I did! He must know some time. If we stand firm
together, we're certain to win.'

'You had no right to tell him!' Urquhart shouted. 'Llewellyn has
great influence. We may be dismissed!' He got up and walked
towards the door. 'You're a nice man, Manson, but you have no
common sense. Good night.'

Medley and Oxborrow followed him, leaving Con and
Andrew alone in the room.

Andrew opened some bottles of drink and, with this to
comfort them, they sat down and discussed the stupidity and
weakness of the other three doctors. They talked for so long that
they did not hear Christine come in and go to bed.

Next morning, Andrew had a bad headache. While walking
down the street to see a patient, he passed Llewellyn in his car.
Llewellyn smiled at him.

Chapter 15   A New Qualification

Andrew felt very miserable. On Sunday morning, while lying in bed, he suddenly shouted at Christine: 'I don't mind about the money! It's the *idea* of making these payments that angers me. Why can't I forget about it? Why don't I like Llewellyn?'

'I think you are jealous of Llewellyn!' said Christine.

'What!' Andrew shouted. 'Why should I be jealous of him?'

'Because he's very good at his work, and – well, because he's a better qualified doctor than you are.'

'God! Now I know what you really think of me!' He jumped out of bed and began to walk about the room. 'What do qualifications matter?'

'Well, love, you don't want to remain here all your life, do you? If you had a good degree, it would help you to get a better post.'

Andrew swung round. 'Chris, you're right!' He thought for a moment. 'But no – it isn't possible! To take a degree, I should have to learn some foreign languages.'

Christine ran up and kissed him. 'You would only need a little knowledge of the languages. And I could help you. Remember: your wife was once a schoolteacher!'

They made plans excitedly all day, and that evening Christine gave Andrew his first lessons. She helped him every evening. Andrew studied to such a late hour each night that when he went to bed he was often too tired to sleep. He lost weight and became thinner in the face. But Chris was always there to comfort and encourage him.

By August, which was a very hot month, Andrew was ready to do some practical work in medicine. This presented another difficulty: where could he get this experience? It was Christine who thought of Challis and his important post at Cardiff University. When Andrew wrote to him, Challis immediately agreed to let him work at the University.

'You were quite right, Chris!' Andrew said. 'It *is* nice to have friends. And I didn't want to go to the Vaughans' that night when we met Challis!'

Andrew bought himself an old motorcycle. There were three afternoon hours during which Andrew was not on duty. So on those days, after lunch, he rode 50 kilometres to Cardiff, worked at the University for one hour, and then rode back again. The work and the long journey in the heat made him so tired that he was almost ill.

At last he had covered every subject in which he would be examined. He went alone to London to sit for his degree. Now that the event was so near, Andrew felt that he knew nothing. But when his examination began, he wrote and wrote, never looking at the clock.

On the second day he was examined by two doctors, in turn, on the practical work of medicine. Andrew found himself fearing this even more than he had feared the written papers. His first examiner, Dr Gadsby, looked at him coldly, and then asked him six questions. Five of these Andrew answered correctly, but the sixth he could not answer. Appearing to lose his patience, Gadsby repeated the question several times. Then, without a word, he passed him on to the second examiner, Sir Robert Abbey.

Andrew crossed the room with a pale face. He felt certain that he had failed already. He raised his eyes, and saw Robert Abbey smiling at him.

'What's the matter?' asked Abbey.

'Nothing, sir,' Andrew answered slowly. 'I don't think that Dr Gadsby was very pleased with my answers – that's all.'

'Don't worry,' Abbey comforted him. Though Abbey was now one of the most famous doctors in Europe, he remembered his own early struggles and therefore felt great sympathy for Andrew.

He began in a friendly manner to question Andrew. His

questions, at first simple, gradually became more difficult. But Andrew, encouraged by Abbey's pleasant manner, answered well.

Abbey then asked him a question about a condition of the body called "aneurism". 'Do you know the history of aneurism?'

'Paré,' Andrew answered, 'is supposed to have been the first man to discover the condition.'

Abbey's face expressed surprise. 'Why do you say "supposed", Dr Manson? Paré *did* discover aneurism.'

Andrew reddened. 'Well, sir, the medical books say so. But I don't think that they're correct. When I was studying for my degree, I read a long description of aneurism in a book that was written 1,300 years before Paré lived!'

Abbey looked at Andrew with a strange expression.

'Dr Manson,' he said, 'you are the first person in an examination who has ever told me something which I did not know. Well done!'

Andrew turned red again.

'Now just answer one more question,' Abbey ended. 'What do you consider the most important rule for a doctor?'

Andrew thought for a moment. 'I suppose – never to believe anything till it is proved.'

'Thank you, Dr Manson.'

At last it was over. At four o'clock in the afternoon Abbey came to him, smiling, and told him that he had passed.

He had done it! He had got his degree! He ran down to the nearest post office and sent a message with the great news to Christine.

Chapter 16   Accident at the Mine

When his train reached Aberalaw, it was nearly midnight. As Andrew was walking home, a miner called Frank Davis ran up to him, crying: 'Doctor – you're wanted!'

'What's wrong?' shouted Andrew.

'There's been an accident at the mine. A man is almost buried under the coal. It's Sam Bevan – one of your patients. Come quickly, Doctor.'

'I shall need my bag,' Andrew said. 'Run to my house and get it. I'll go straight to the mine.'

Andrew reached the mine in four minutes. The manager and three men were waiting for him.

'It's a terrible accident,' said the manager. 'Nobody has been killed, but one of the men is trapped. We can't move him! And there's a danger that more coal will fall.'

At that moment, Davis ran up to them with his bag. Without delay, the small party began to go slowly down into the deep and dangerous mine. The passage to the mine was so narrow that Andrew and the other four men had to creep forward on their hands and knees for nearly a kilometre. At last, they reached the scene of the accident.

'Here's the doctor. Get back, and give him room to move,' the manager ordered the three men who had been trying to get Bevan out.

They pulled themselves back, and Andrew crept forward.

Bevan tried to smile at Manson. 'Well, I'm giving you a good chance to test your skill!'

By the light of the manager's lamp, Andrew examined the trapped man. The whole of Bevan's body was free except for his left arm, which was buried under a heavy pile of coal and badly damaged. Andrew saw at once that the only way to free Bevan was to cut off his arm.

Bevan read Andrew's decision in his face. 'Go on, then, Doctor,' he said bravely. 'Cut it off – I can bear it. Just get me out of here as quickly as you can!'

'Don't worry, Sam.' Andrew said. 'I'm going to put you to

sleep now. When you wake up, you will be in bed.'

Kneeling in a pool of water, Andrew took off his coat and placed it under Bevan's head. Then he opened his bag. But he was shocked to discover that the bottle that he needed was broken! He could not put Bevan to sleep. Andrew trembled. For perhaps 30 seconds, he could not decide what to do. Then he quickly pulled out another bottle and gave Bevan something to reduce the pain.

'Shut your eyes, Sam!' he said.

As the knife cut into him, Bevan gave a loud cry of pain. He cried out again. Then, when the knife touched the bone, he fainted.

Andrew could not see what he was doing in this hole, deep down beneath the ground. He had never worked in such difficult conditions before. He would never be able to cut through the bone! At any moment the coal would crash down on them and kill them all! Oh, God, would he never finish?

In the end, he almost cried with relief. He put a bandage over the wound, and, lifting himself onto his knees, said: 'Take him out.'

Forty-five metres away, with more room to move and four lamps round him, he treated the wound more thoroughly. Finished!

'Wrap him up warmly,' Andrew ordered the miners.

Slowly, gently, they carried Bevan out of the mine. When they had struggled along for about 55 metres, they heard a long, loud crash of falling coal in the darkness behind them. 'That's it!' the manager said to Andrew.

It took them nearly an hour to reach the surface. There they found a crowd of women, waiting anxiously. Suddenly, Andrew heard a voice desperately calling his name. The next moment, Christine threw her arms round his neck, crying loudly.

'What's the matter?' Andrew asked, surprised.

Holding on to him like a drowning woman, she said: 'They

told us that the coal had crashed down on you – that you wouldn't, couldn't, come out alive!'

Chapter 17   Christmas

The saving of Sam Bevan greatly increased Andrew's popularity. He received smiles from people who had taken no notice of him before. Medical cards began to come back to him.

Owen was delighted, 'Didn't I tell you that this would happen?' he said.

Andrew's new degree also improved his position in the town. Denny, now abroad, did not yet know about his success. But Freddie Hamson wrote to Andrew to say how pleased he was.

'It's a pity that we never see Freddie nowadays.' Andrew remarked to Christine. 'Hasn't he written a nice letter?'

'Yes, very nice – but most of it is about himself!' Christine replied.

The next few weeks passed very happily. On the evening before Christmas, Andrew returned home from the surgery with a pleasant feeling of peace and goodwill. As he entered the house, he saw at once that Christine had the same feeling.

'Shut your eyes and come with me!' she said, holding out her hand.

She led him into the kitchen, where, on the table, lay a number of packages, each with a little note. Andrew realized at once that these were presents from his patients.

'Look, Andrew!' Christine cried. 'A chicken and two ducks! And a lovely cake! And a bottle of wine! Isn't it kind of them? Isn't it nice that they *want* to give you these presents?'

For a moment he could not speak. This generous sign that the people of Aberalaw had begun to like him touched him deeply.

Walking up and down the kitchen, he said: 'That's how poor

people should always pay their doctor, Chris. No money, no bills! If a patient is poor, let him give the doctor something that he can afford. If every doctor stopped thinking about how much money he could make, the whole system would be better.'

'Yes, dear.'

Next morning, Christmas Day, was fine and bright. After breakfast, Andrew went out to see his patients. Dinners were cooking in all the little houses, and his own was cooking at home. In every street, people called out: 'Happy Christmas, Doctor!' Their cheerful behaviour, so different from that of a year ago, made Andrew very happy.

Except for Chenkin, whom he did not want, the only patient who had not come back to him was Tom Evans. Andrew suddenly decided to call on Evans and wish him a happy Christmas. After knocking once, he opened the front door and walked straight into the kitchen. There, he had a shock. The kitchen was almost empty; and Evans was sitting on a broken chair in front of a miserable fire that gave no heat. On his knee sat his little girl, who was four years old.

Suddenly Evans turned and saw Andrew. An expression of shame and anger spread across his face. Andrew saw that Evans was ashamed at being found in such a state by the doctor whose advice he had refused. Andrew felt sad and awkward; he wanted to turn and go away. But, at that moment, Mrs Evans entered the kitchen.

She was so surprised to see Andrew that she cried out: 'What's the matter, sir? He hasn't done anything wrong, has he?'

'Mrs Evans,' Andrew replied, looking down at the floor, 'I would like us to be friends. It's Christmas, and – well, I would be so pleased if the three of you would come round and help us to eat our Christmas dinner.'

'But, Doctor–' she began.

'You be quiet!' Evans interrupted her angrily. 'We don't

want help from anybody!'

'What do you mean? I'm inviting you as a friend,' said Andrew.

'Eat your Christmas dinner yourself!' Evans shouted. 'We don't want it.'

Andrew turned to Mrs Evans. 'You persuade him, Mrs Evans. I shall be really sorry if you don't come. We'll expect you at half past one.'

Before either of them could reply, he left the house.

The Evans family arrived, washed and brushed and looking very uncomfortable. At first it seemed as if the Christmas dinner would be a failure. But then, by good fortune, Andrew accidentally upset his soup on to the table. There was a silence. Then the little girl burst out laughing. The next minute, they were all laughing.

After the meal, Christine led Mrs Evans and the child into the living room, leaving Andrew alone with Evans. The two men sat in silence for a time. Then Andrew said: 'I'm sorry about your arm, Tom.'

'You're not as sorry as I am,' Evans replied.

There was a pause. Then Andrew continued: 'Will you allow me to speak to Mr Vaughan about you? I have a little influence with him, and I feel certain that I could persuade him to find you some easier work to do.'

Evans did not answer. He said nothing. He was in tears; his whole body was shaking.

At half past three the Evans family left and Christine and Andrew went into the living room.

'You know, Chris,' Andrew said, 'that poor man lost the use of his arm because of Oxborrow. He's the man to blame! When Evans left me, he went to Oxborrow who gave him the wrong treatment. Oxborrow knows nothing – nothing! There ought to be a law to–'

'Andrew, dear!' Christine smiled at him from her chair. 'Do stop talking about your work. I want to tell you something important!'

'Yes?'

She laughed silently. 'Come over here.'

He sat on the chair beside her. 'Well? What is this great news?'

She gave another little laugh. 'Andrew – I'm going to have a baby.'

'A baby? Really? You mean . . .'

'Yes. I've been trying to tell you all day.'

Chapter 18   The Rotten Bridge

Spring came again. The garden was bright with the flowers that Christine had planted in the autumn. Now Andrew would allow her to do no more work. 'You've made the garden. Now sit in it,' he ordered her.

Excited at the thought of becoming a father, Andrew suddenly decided to ask Dr Llewellyn to attend his wife at the birth of the baby.

Llewellyn, when Andrew telephoned him, seemed pleased. 'I shall be glad to help you, Manson. I didn't think that you liked me enough to ask me to do this. I promise to do my best. For now, I think that it would do your wife good to have a short holiday.'

Acting on Llewellyn's advice, Christine went to stay with an aunt. Andrew missed her even more than he had expected to do. He spent one or two evenings with the Bolands and the Vaughans, but most evenings he continued with his research into coal dust.

He made a discovery which excited him greatly. Standing in

front of the dead fire, long after midnight, he suddenly seized Christine's photograph and cried: 'Chris! I believe that I am going to do something important!'

Christine returned at the end of June. 'Oh, it is nice to be home again!' she said, throwing her arms round him. Then, as she looked into his face, her expression changed. 'Andrew, dear, you look tired! I don't believe that you have been eating properly.' She was worried about him.

Andrew told her about the developments in his research.

'How long is this going to take you?' she asked.

'I don't know. It may take a year, or it may take five years!'

'Well, in that case, you will have to work to a system – keep regular hours, and not stay up too late, wearing yourself out!'

'There's nothing the matter with me.'

But Christine was firm. Every evening, while Andrew worked, she sat in his work room, reading. Then, at 11 o'clock, she would rise from her chair and say: 'Time for bed!'

'Oh – not yet! You go up, Chris! I'll follow you in a minute.'

'Andrew Manson, if you think that I'm going to bed alone *in my state of health*!'

These last words, a joke about the baby that she was expecting, always ended the argument. With a laugh, he would stretch himself and put away his microscope.

Towards the end of July, Andrew became particularly busy with his practice. One afternoon, as he walked up the road feeling very tired, he saw Dr Llewellyn's car outside his gate. Thinking that perhaps the baby had been born early, he ran home, burst into the house, and said eagerly: 'Hullo, Llewellyn. I – I didn't expect to see you here so soon.'

'No,' Llewellyn answered.

Andrew smiled. 'Well?'

Llewellyn did not smile. 'I have been trying to find you all morning,' he said.

'Is anything wrong?'

Llewellyn looked through the window towards the old bridge in the garden. 'Manson,' he said gently. 'This morning, when your wife was walking over that bridge, a piece of wood broke. She fell. She is all right – quite all right. But I am afraid that the baby . . .'

Andrew understood even before Llewellyn finished.

'We did everything that we could,' Llewellyn continued in a voice of deep sympathy. 'I came at once, and brought a nurse from the hospital. We've been here all day.'

There was silence. Andrew covered his eyes with his hands and cried to himself.

'Nobody is to blame. It was an accident,' Llewellyn tried to comfort him. 'Now go upstairs and see your wife.'

His head lowered, Andrew went upstairs. Outside the door of the bedroom he paused, breathing heavily. Then he went inside.

Chapter 19   Experiments

By the year 1927, opinions about Dr Manson were rather mixed in Aberalaw. His practice was not large, but all his patients had the greatest confidence in him. He rarely gave medicines, but when he did do so he gave the newest, best, and often the most expensive medicines on the market. By his use of modern medicines, Manson once prevented a serious disease from spreading through the town, although the rest of the area suffered badly.

The committee of the Medical Society ought to have been grateful to Manson; but a few of its members, led by Chenkin, were jealous of his success. Though Manson had many friends, he also had enemies.

Andrew sometimes asked himself why he and Christine had

remained in Aberalaw after the death of their child. His coal dust research was the only reason for staying: he could not leave the mines until he had completed that.

He now had a great deal of important information about the effect of coal dust on the miners' lungs. But, in order to prove his facts, he decided to do a few tests on small animals, to study the action of the dust on their lungs. Here, his real troubles began. Taking care to cause the animals as little pain as possible, Andrew did some extremely successful tests, which proved all his beliefs. He felt proud and excited. But then, a few days later, he had a shock.

When Andrew returned home from work, he found Christine looking worried. 'What's the matter?' he asked her.

She looked at him unhappily. 'I had some visitors today.'

'Oh? Who were they?'

'Five members of the committee, including Chenkin. They had heard about your tests on the animals, and wanted to see your work room. I told them that you were not at home; but they pushed me out of the way and rushed into your room. When they saw what was in there, one of the men shouted: "Oh, the poor animals!" I tried to tell them that they had not suffered, but they refused to listen. They put the animals in a bag and took them away.'

'What!' Andrew shouted. He thought for a minute, and then went into the hall to use the telephone. But, just as he reached it, the telephone bell rang. 'Hullo!' he said angrily. Then his voice changed. It was Owen. 'Look here, Owen–'

'I know, I know,' Owen interrupted. 'This is a bad business. I'll come along to see you now.'

Owen came. Before Andrew could speak, he said: 'Did you get permission?'

Andrew looked at him in surprise. 'Permission for what?'

'To do tests on animals.'

'Good heavens, no! I never thought about it!'

'I'm afraid that there will be trouble,' Owen said. 'Some members of the committee feel very bitter about you. But don't worry: everything will be all right in the end.'

Owen went away. The following evening, Andrew received a letter ordering him to attend an inquiry to be held by the committee a week later.

The news that there was to be an inquiry caused a lot of discussion in Aberalaw. Fights broke out between Andrew's friends and his enemies. Andrew himself felt tired, angry and worried.

On Sunday afternoon, he presented himself before the committee. A large crowd was waiting in the street when Andrew entered the offices and walked up the narrow stairs to the committee room, which also was packed with people.

The inquiry began with an angry speech by Chenkin, who shouted that Andrew had broken the law by doing tests on animals without permission and should be reported for this crime.

Here, Owen interrupted. 'I must warn the committee that if we report Dr Manson for this, the whole committee may run into trouble.'

'What do you mean?' Chenkin asked.

'As Dr Manson is employed by us,' Owen explained, 'we are responsible in law for his actions!'

There were cries of: 'Owen's right! We don't want any trouble!'

'Never mind about the permission, then!' shouted Chenkin. 'There are many other complaints against him.'

'Yes! Yes!' someone at the back called out. 'Remember all those afternoons that he wasted, riding about on his motorcycle!'

'He won't give medicines!' came another voice.

'All these complaints,' Chenkin shouted, 'prove that Dr Manson has served us badly. We demand that he gives up his job.'

Chenkin looked round at his friends and sat down to loud cheers.

'Perhaps you will now allow Dr Manson to speak,' Owen said, and turned to Andrew.

There was a silence. Andrew sat still for a moment. The situation was worse than he had expected. He rose to his feet.

He was not a good speaker, but he was angry now. He began: 'What I have been doing wasn't cruel. Why do you men take mice and birds down the mines? To see if gas is present! When these mice and birds are killed by the gas, do you call that cruelty? No – of course you don't! You realize that these tests with animals save men's lives – *your* lives. Well, that is what I have been trying to do for you! For three years I have been doing research into the diseases that you get from the dust in the mines. I have made a discovery that may improve your conditions of work – a discovery that will keep you in good health better than bottles of medicine can do! You don't believe me! You think that I lie to you! But this will show you what other people think of my experiments – people who are able to judge.'

He took a letter from his pocket and handed it to Owen. It was from a university in Scotland, offering him another medical degree in recognition of his important coal dust discoveries.

Owen read the letter, gave a sudden smile of relief, and then passed it round to the members of the committee. After a few more remarks, he said: 'Perhaps you will leave us now, Doctor, please.'

When Andrew returned to the committee room, everyone, except for Chenkin, seemed to be more friendly.

Owen stood up and said: 'I'm glad to tell you, Dr Manson, that the committee has decided to ask you to remain.'

He had won! But his victory gave Andrew no satisfaction. The committee expected him to be pleased. But, instead, he said: 'Thank you, Mr Owen. I'm glad that the committee wishes me to stay, but I am afraid that I cannot do so. I give the committee a month's notice from today.' He spoke without feeling, and then walked out of the room.

There was silence. Then Chenkin called out: 'He'll be no loss!'

Owen now lost his temper. 'Be quiet, Chenkin,' he shouted. 'We have lost the best man we've ever had.'

Chapter 20   An Offer of Work

Andrew woke up in the middle of that night, calling out: 'Am I a fool, Chris?'

She comforted him in the darkness. 'No. We don't want to stay in Wales for the rest of our lives, dear. We've been happy here, but it's time for us to move on.'

'But Chris, we can't afford to buy a practice yet. We ought to save some more money before we leave here.'

'What does money matter?' she answered in a sleepy voice.

Her confidence gave him courage. Next morning the world seemed a cheerful place. He had no need to worry about the risk that he was taking! He now had a degree and over three hundred pounds in the bank. They would never be hungry.

Now that he was to leave, everybody wanted him to stay. A week after the inquiry, Owen and two or three members of the committee called at his house and asked Andrew to change his mind. But he refused.

Reports of his coal dust discoveries had recently been printed in a number of medical papers in England and America. A few days later, as a result of these reports, Andrew received several letters.

One letter was from Challis, who asked Andrew to visit him that week. Andrew lost the letter and forgot to answer it. Another letter interested him more.

'This pleases me, Chris! It's from an American named Stillman,' he told her.

'Yes? Is he a doctor?' she asked.

'No – not really. He runs a small hospital in America, where he treats people for diseases of the lung. The medical profession refuses to recognize him. But Stillman is a good man – very clever at his work. I'll tell you about him some time.'

He sat down and replied to Stillman immediately.

As he still neglected to answer Challis, Andrew soon received a second letter from him. This stated that the Coal and Mines Board, having read about his coal dust experiments, wished Andrew to be their Medical Officer.

When Christine read the letter, she said happily: 'Didn't I tell you that something like this would happen? Isn't it good?'

'Yes, lovely!'

Andrew went straight to the post office and sent a message to Challis accepting the offer.

Chapter 21   The Coal and Mines Board

The offices of the Coal and Mines Board were in a large stone building in the centre of London. On a bright morning in August, Andrew ran up the steps of this building in high spirits.

'I'm the new Medical Officer,' he told the man at the door.

'Yes, sir,' said the man. 'Mr Gill is expecting you. Jones! Take our new doctor to Mr Gill's room.'

Andrew was led into a large, sunny room where Mr Gill, a cheerful little man, shook hands with him and said: 'Please sit down. Would you like a cup of tea?'

While they drank their tea, Gill made some remarks about the weather. Then he led Andrew to his room, which was also sunny with a view of the river. 'I – I hope you will like this room,' Gill said with a smile.

'Oh, yes – it's a beautiful room!'

'Now I'll introduce you to your secretary – Miss Mason.' Gill took him into the next room, where Miss Mason, a friendly young woman, sat at a small desk.

'Miss Mason, this is Dr Manson.'

'Good morning, Dr Manson.'

They had a short conversation, and then Andrew returned to his own room, where Gill remarked: 'I'll send you some reports to read.'

A pile of reports arrived. Andrew read these dull accounts of meetings of the Board as quickly as he could, and then went to Gill and asked: 'When can I start work?'

Gill was surprised at his question. 'Heavens, have you read those reports already? I thought that I had given you enough to keep you busy for a month!' He looked at his watch. 'Let's go out. It's time for lunch.'

At lunch, Gill explained that the Board would not meet again till the middle of September, and that there would be no other work for Andrew until after that meeting.

Andrew went back to Christine that evening with a feeling of disappointment. 'Would you believe it, Chris?' he said. 'They're not *ready* for me! For a whole month I shall have nothing to do except to read reports and drink tea!'

'Never mind!' said Christine, her thoughts on other things. 'It's lovely here – much nicer than Aberalaw. I went for a walk this afternoon. Oh! I planned such lovely things for us to do.' He had rarely seen her so excited. 'My love, let's go out to dinner! Then, if you're not too tired, we might go to the theatre.'

As she led him to the door, he laughed. 'I need some

entertainment after my first day's hard work.'

Next morning, he read every report again. Then he began to explore the building. Suddenly he found himself in a long room, where a young man in a dirty white coat was sitting on a box, smoking a pipe and doing nothing.

'Hullo!' Andrew said.

The other answered tiredly: 'Lost your way?'

Andrew introduced himself. 'My name's Manson.'

'I thought so. So you've come to join the forgotten men!' He paused. 'I'm Dr Hope.'

'What are you doing here?'

'Heaven knows! Some of the time I sit here and think. But most of the time I just sit. Occasionally, when there has been an explosion, they send me bits of a dead miner to examine, and tell me to find out the cause of the accident.'

They went out to lunch together. Hope then told Andrew more about his duties, and about the members of the Board, three of whom were Challis, Abbey and Gadsby.

'Do you know Gadsby?' Hope asked.

'I've met the gentleman!' Andrew told Hope about his examination.

'Gadsby is a clever man – but he's only interested in himself.' Hope, who had a great sense of fun, laughed suddenly and then told Andrew a joke that Abbey had once made about Gadsby. He gave another loud laugh and then became serious. 'Abbey is the best man on the Board. The others spend so much time quarrelling that they never make any decisions!'

Andrew and Hope had lunch together nearly every day. Although Hope was always joking, he was a clever young man. Andrew believed that, one day, he might do something important.

While Andrew waited for the next meeting of the Board, he

and Christine explored London. They began to feel that they belonged there.

Chapter 22   Measuring Bandages

At last, on the afternoon of September 18th, the Board met. Sitting beside Gill and Hope, Andrew watched the members enter the long room.

'Gentlemen!' the President addressed the meeting. 'We are pleased to welcome our new Medical Officer. Dr Manson has made some important discoveries, and we must give him every opportunity to develop his research. We wish him, gentlemen, to visit the mines and examine the miners in many parts of the country. We will give him all the help that we can – including the skilled services of our young friend Dr Hope.'

Andrew drew one quick breath. This was better than he had expected.

'But, gentlemen,' the President continued, 'before Dr Manson starts this work, I think that he should attend to another and more urgent matter. I think that, first, he should make a study of the medical materials used for accidents in mines. For example, there is no fixed standard for the width of bandages. I feel that Dr Manson should inquire into this matter, and make a report, suggesting the best width and length of bandage for each of the most common forms of accident.'

Silence. Andrew looked desperately round the table.

'Surely, sir, this – this bandage question is of little importance,' Abbey argued. 'Dr Manson–'

'It is certainly not of little importance! The Government has asked for this report.'

'Excuse me, sir,' Andrew interrupted. 'I – I understood that

I was to do medical work here. For a month I have been wasting my time doing nothing. Now, if you expect me to ...'

He stopped, and looked at them. It was Abbey who helped him.

'Dr Manson's argument is very reasonable. For four years he has worked patiently at his research; and now, after offering him the opportunity to work on this further, you want to send him out to measure bandages!'

'If Dr Manson has been patient for four years, he can be patient for a little longer!' the President laughed.

After the meeting, Andrew discussed the matter with Gill and Hope.

'It won't take you long – only about six months,' Gill comforted him. 'Then you can begin your work on the coal dust.'

'He won't get the chance!' Hope laughed. 'He'll be measuring bandages for the rest of his life!'

'Oh, very funny!' Andrew picked up his hat and went home to Christine.

He bought an old car; and on the following Monday, he and Christine began their tour of the coal mines. 'Anyway, at least we are together, Chris!' Andrew remarked.

The work was very simple. Andrew examined the medical supplies at several hundred mines, and then returned to London and wrote his report.

The Coal and Mines Board sent this report to an important member of the Government, who at once asked Andrew to call at his office.

'Your report is excellent, Manson,' he told him. 'The Government intends to introduce a new law controlling the use of medical supplies in mines and factories. We shall base this law on your report. But there is one suggestion that I would like you to change. I think that a narrower bandage would be better than the size you suggest. Don't you agree?'

Andrew was angry. 'Personally, I prefer the bigger bandage – but I really don't think that it makes much difference!'

'What? *No difference?*'

'No – no difference at all!'

'You treat this matter very lightly. Don't you realize how important this is?'

Andrew lost his temper. 'Have you ever been down a mine? I have. I've done a bloody operation, lying in a pool of water with only one small lamp and no room to move. And I tell you this: the size of the bandage is of no importance.'

Andrew left the building more quickly than he had entered. When he returned to his office at the Coal and Mines Board, he stood for some time, looking out of the window. 'I don't belong here,' he thought. 'I'm a doctor – not a clerk!'

Towards the end of May, he informed the Board that he was leaving.

Gill tried to persuade him to stay. But Hope said: 'Don't listen to him! You're lucky. I shall leave as soon as I can find another post – if I don't go mad first!'

Several months later the Government, acting on information supplied by Dr Gadsby, publicly declared that coal dust was the cause of a dangerous disease. Next day, the newspapers praised Gadsby for his useful work and described him as a great doctor!

Chapter 23   Andrew's First Practice

Andrew and Christine began to search for a practice. They sold their car to add to their savings. They now had six hundred pounds, but it appeared that this was not enough money with which to buy a practice in London. Then, when they had almost lost hope, Andrew heard that a doctor in the Paddington area of

London had died, and that his practice was for sale at a price which they could just afford.

When they went to see the large, cold house that would be their home, they were disappointed.

'It's in a miserable area,' said Andrew. Then, suddenly becoming more cheerful, he added: 'But there are nice houses in the neighbourhood. What do you think, Chris? Shall we take a chance, and buy it?'

Christine was doubtful. She was tired of London now. She hated this cold house and the dirty streets. She wanted to go back to the country. But Andrew seemed so anxious to buy a practice in London that she let him have his wish. 'All right,' she said. 'Buy the practice if you would like to.'

He bought the practice; and in October he and Christine moved into their new home.

'We've spent everything, Chris. You must be very careful with the money,' Andrew warned her.

To his surprise, she burst into tears. '*Careful!* Aren't I always careful?'

'Chris! What's the matter with you?'

'Oh, I hate this house! It's so dark and dirty! I–'

'But, Chris, it's the practice that's important – not the house!' He held her in his arms and tried to comfort her.

Next morning, at nine o'clock, he opened his surgery. His heart was beating fast with excitement. Half past nine came. He waited anxiously. It was nearly 11 o'clock now, and still no patient had arrived.

Suddenly the surgery bell rang, and an old woman walked in. She had a bad cough. Andrew examined her, and then gave her a bottle of medicine, for which she paid him a small amount.

Andrew felt as excited as if this was the first money that he had ever earned. He ran to Christine, and showed her the coins. 'First patient, Chris! This money will buy our lunch!'

That evening, three patients came to his surgery. But, on the following day, he received no patients; and on the next day he earned less than a pound.

Andrew began to ask himself if he had made a bad mistake in buying this practice. He and Christine were so poor that sometimes they did not have enough to eat. They went to a cheap food shop, owned by a fat little German woman who called herself Mrs Smith, for their meals.

Mrs Smith liked them and was kind to them. She became very fond of Christine, and one day she said to Andrew: 'You will be all right. You will succeed. You have a good wife. Don't worry – I will send you patients.'

They tried to pretend that their struggles were amusing; but never had they known such hard times.

Chapter 24   Andrew Decides to Succeed

Andrew felt a great desire for the friendship of another doctor. Denny was abroad, having taken a post with an oil company, and Hope was now working in the north of England. So Andrew decided to telephone Freddie Hamson.

'This is Manson – Andrew Manson. I've bought a practice in London,' he told him.

'Manson! In London! Good heavens, man! Why didn't you telephone me before?'

'Oh, I've been too busy!' Andrew smiled to himself. 'I'm married now, Freddie.'

'So am I! We must meet at once. Can you come to dinner on Thursday? Good!'

Christine expressed no pleasure when Andrew told her of the invitation.

'You go alone, Andrew,' she suggested.

'Oh nonsense! I know that you don't like Freddie very much, but there'll be other people there as well – probably other doctors.'

When they arrived at Hamson's grand house on Thursday night, Freddie greeted them most warmly. 'It's lovely to see you people again. How do you like my house, old man? Didn't I tell you that I would succeed?'

It looked a most expensive house. Andrew was about to express his admiration when Mrs Hamson entered. Almost at once, the other guests arrived. Introductions followed, with much talk and laughter. Then they went into dinner, a good meal with expensive food and drink.

After two glasses of wine, Andrew felt very happy. He listened with interest when Ivory and Deedman, two well-known and successful doctors, talked loudly about their medical experiences. He said to himself: 'I must get to know these men better. They're so rich and successful!'

'I played a clever trick the other day,' said Ivory. 'I persuaded a patient to have a course of 12 treatments. I told him that the usual charge for this was fifty pounds, but that I would be willing to reduce the price to forty-five pounds if he paid me immediately. He gave me a cheque at once!'

'That's the way to make money!' Freddie laughed. 'And a bottle of medicine would have done him just as much good!'

Ivory smiled. 'Yes – and the price of the medicine is under a pound!'

'Most people,' remarked Deedman, 'do not realize how little these treatments really cost. The important thing is to make them *think* that they are expensive!'

Ivory and Hamson agreed. 'Exactly! The more you charge a patient, the more confidence he has in you!'

They continued to talk in this manner after dinner. Andrew listened, smoked and drank. They all drank. They brought

Andrew into their conversation, and when Christine said that it was time to go home Ivory remarked warmly: 'If at any time you would like my advice about a case, Manson, let me know. I shall always be pleased to help you.'

Andrew thanked him, and walked with an unsteady step to the door.

On their way home, he said happily: 'Chris! We've had a lovely time, haven't we?'

She answered coldly: 'We've had a terrible time! I like Denny and Hope – but not those people!'

'Why? What do you mean? What's wrong with–'

'Everything! The food, the furniture, the way they talked – money is all that they think about!'

Mistaking her remark for jealousy, Andrew cried out: 'I'll make money for you, Chris!'

'I don't want money!' she said.

'But, my dear–' He tried to put his arm round her.

'Don't! I love you, Andrew – but not when you've drunk too much!'

Andrew said no more, but when he went to bed that night he promised himself: 'I *will* make money! I'm going to succeed, too!'

Next morning, Andrew looked up the qualifications of Ivory, Deedman and Hamson in a medical book. To his surprise, he discovered that these rich doctors did not have the qualifications he did. 'I can do better than they are doing!' he said to himself.

Andrew made a sudden decision to find himself a part-time post at a London hospital. As such appointments were not easy to find, he went to see Sir Robert Abbey.

'I will do my best to help you,' Abbey promised him. 'The Victoria Chest Hospital would be the best for you. I will make some inquiries.'

Andrew went home, feeling very pleased.

'I've just seen Abbey,' he told Christine. 'He's going to try to get me a post at the Victoria Hospital. A hospital appointment would improve my position greatly.'

The pleasure in her eyes made him feel sorry. 'I've been very bad-tempered recently, Chris! Will you forgive me?' he asked.

She ran to him, saying that it had been her fault.

Andrew now worked with increased determination, feeling sure that he would soon have some good luck. Slowly his practice improved. But he still had many disappointments. Some of his cases were serious, needing admission to hospital at once. Yet Andrew could rarely persuade any hospital to admit even the most dangerous case. 'Dr Who?' they would ask when he telephoned. 'Who? No, no! Sorry! We have no empty beds!'

One day Andrew went to Christine, complaining. 'They've plenty of beds for their own doctors. If they don't know a doctor, they refuse to admit his patients. This is London! This is our hospital system! It's terrible!'

He was still waiting to hear from Abbey about the hospital appointment. He was also disappointed that he had not heard from Hamson or his friends since their dinner. Feeling rather miserable, he sat in his surgery one evening towards the end of April, thinking about his future. It was nearly nine o'clock, and he was about to lock the door for the night when a young woman entered.

'What is your trouble?' he asked her.

She smiled and sat down. 'Mrs Smith, in the little food shop, advised me to come to you, Doctor,' she said. 'I work at a large dress shop. My name is Miss Cramb. I am having trouble with my hands. I have been to several doctors in this area, but they have not been able to cure me.'

He looked at her hands, which were very red and sore. With sudden interest, he examined them more closely.

'They make it difficult for me to work,' she said. 'I've tried various medicines, but they have done no good.'

'No. They wouldn't,' he said. 'You are suffering from a rather rare skin disease. Medicines are useless for this disease. It is caused by the food you eat.'

'Well, no doctor has told me that before!'

He laughed and wrote out a list of the foods that she must avoid.

She took the list saying: 'I'll take your advice, Doctor. I'll try anything!' She paid Andrew for his services, and left.

Ten days later, she returned. 'Look at my hands now, Doctor. Cured! I am so grateful to you!'

'That's all right,' Andrew answered awkwardly.

She rose. 'Perhaps one day I shall be able to prove to you that I am grateful,' she said.

He smiled and showed her to the door.

Chapter 25   New Patients

Miss Cramb's cure caused surprise and excitement at her dress shop. She advised the other girls working there to go to Andrew; and they all took her advice. Anxious to see what this great doctor was like, at least six or seven girls who had nothing really the matter with them attended his surgery every evening. Their visits greatly increased Andrew's profits. But Miss Cramb was only beginning to express her thanks.

In the first week of June, Andrew received a letter asking him to call at the home of a Miss Everett, a rich woman who lived in a very expensive part of London. 'This is my chance — at last!' he told himself when, closing his surgery early, he left home to visit Miss Everett.

The servant who opened the door led him into a large, beautifully decorated room where Miss Everett, a woman of about fifty, was waiting for him. She gave him one look and then came straight to the point.

'My doctor has died. It's a pity, because I trusted him completely. Miss Cramb suggested you to me. I looked up your qualifications. You're well qualified!' She paused and took another look at him. 'I think that, perhaps, you might be the doctor for me. I always have treatment for hay fever at this time of year. You understand hay fever, I suppose?'

'Yes,' he answered. 'Which treatment do you have?'

She mentioned the name of a well-known cure. 'My last doctor advised it. It has been very helpful.'

Andrew wanted to tell her that this treatment was useless, but decided that this would be foolish. He could not risk losing this chance to make money! He said: 'Then I will give you the same treatment, Miss Everett.'

'Good! I suggest that I pay you a pound for each visit. Do you agree to this arrangement?'

A pound a visit! He had never been paid so much before! The idea of giving a treatment in which he did not believe no longer worried him. What did it matter if it was useless? He was tired of failure. He wanted to succeed. And he would succeed!

He visited Miss Everett again the following day at 11 o'clock. He then called twice a week. After each treatment, they would talk together for perhaps half an hour. Andrew told Miss Everett of his desire for success, and she encouraged him.

On his last visit, she gave him a glass of wine and paid him a cheque for twelve pounds for his services. She then led him to the front door, and stood for a moment, looking at him. 'Will you take the advice of a woman who is old enough to be your mother?' she said. 'Get yourself a good suit. You say that you wish to succeed. You will never be successful in those clothes!'

He walked down the road, feeling hurt and angry. But his annoyance soon passed. 'She's quite right,' he thought. 'How can

I attract high-class patients if I wear clothes like these?'

When he reached home, he excitedly showed Christine his cheque. 'Look at that, woman! This is real money – what a well-qualified doctor ought to earn! Twelve pounds just for talking nicely to Miss Everett and giving her the E-treatment!'

'What's that?' she asked, smiling. Then suddenly she was doubtful. 'Haven't I heard you say that that treatment is useless?'

His expression changed. She had made the one remark that he did not wish to hear. 'You're never satisfied!' he shouted, and went out of the room.

The next day he went to a good shop and bought himself two new suits of clothes.

He felt a little awkward when, for the first time, he came down to breakfast wearing one of these suits. Christine was pouring out his coffee when he appeared. For a moment, she was too surprised to speak.

'Andrew!' she cried. 'You look lovely! Are you going somewhere?'

'Going somewhere? I'm going to visit my patients, of course! . . . Well, do you like it?'

'Yes, It's – it's very nice. But . . .' She smiled. 'But it makes you look so strange!'

'You prefer me to dress badly, do you?'

He finished in silence, and then left the room to start his work.

Three weeks later, he had reason to be glad that he had bought these suits, because Miss Everett then sent for him to attend a relative and a friend, both of whom wanted the same hay fever treatment. Andrew gave them the treatment without feeling at all guilty. Actually, he felt very pleased with himself. He was winning! His desire for success made him forget the bitter things that he used to say about other doctors who behaved in this way. He forgot, too, that this improvement in his affairs had been started by a fat little German woman in a cheap food shop.

75

Soon another exciting opportunity was offered to him. One afternoon, when he was counting the money that he had earned during the last month, the telephone rang.

'Oh, Dr Manson,' said a voice, 'this is Mr Winch, the manager of the dress shop in which your patient, Miss Cramb, works. A lady has been taken ill in the shop. Will you come at once, please?'

'I'll be there in four minutes,' Andrew promised him.

He was met at the shop by Miss Cramb, who explained: 'It's Miss le Roy. I advised Mr Winch to send for you.'

At that moment, Mr Winch himself appeared. 'Oh, Doctor, I'm so pleased to see you! Come this way, Doctor.' He led Andrew into a small room, where Miss le Roy was lying on the floor, shouting and crying. She was about twenty-four, with blue eyes and fair hair.

Andrew knelt down beside her. On the other side of her knelt another woman. 'Oh, Toppy, Toppy,' the woman kept saying.

'This is a serious case,' Andrew said. 'Can you get me a chair, please.'

Slowly and very gently, Andrew lifted Miss le Roy, who was still shouting, on to the chair. He held her head, and said a few words quietly to her. Then suddenly he hit her on the face. Immediately, Toppy stopped shouting. Andrew hit her a second time.

Then he turned to her friend and explained. 'Sorry! It was the only thing to do. She might have done herself harm if she had continued like that for any longer. She'll be all right in a few minutes.'

'I must take her home,' said her friend. 'Will you come with us?'

'Very well,' Andrew agreed.

They took Miss le Roy home by car. Her house surprised Andrew: he had never entered such a grand building before!

Toppy threw herself down on to a comfortable chair and said to her friend: 'Ring the bell, dear. I want a drink. Thank heavens Father isn't at home!'

A servant brought in some drinks. When he had gone, Toppy's friend smiled at Andrew and said: 'I'm Mrs Lawrence. I think that I had better explain what happened, Doctor. Toppy had an argument about a dress that she had ordered. She's been feeling very tired of late, and is rather quick to quarrel.' She paused. 'We are very grateful to you, Doctor.'

Toppy looked at Andrew. 'I went mad, Doctor, didn't I? Go on, Doctor – say that I went mad! Laugh! It was very funny!'

'I didn't think it funny!' Andrew spoke quickly, feeling that he, too, should explain himself. 'You had a bad attack. I am sorry that I had to hit you.'

There was a pause. Andrew had finished his drink. 'Well,' he said awkwardly, 'I must get back to my work. Send for your own doctor tomorrow. Goodbye.'

Mrs Lawrence led him into the hall. She was tall, dark, and quite young. She gave him her hand, and said with a smile: 'I admired your form of treatment. I can see that one day you will be a great success!'

Walking down the street, Andrew noticed to his surprise that it was nearly five o'clock. He had spent three hours in the company of these two women. He would be able to charge a high price for his services – a very high price!

Chapter 26   The Nursing Home

On the following morning, when Andrew was about to visit some of his poor patients, Mrs Lawrence telephoned and asked him, in a most friendly manner, to call on Toppy again.

Andrew went straight to the house. Here he met Mr le Roy,

who looked at him quickly and said: 'Listen, Doctor, I'm in a hurry! You're a clever young man! Well then, cure my girl. Stop all her stupid nonsense – her crying and shouting about nothing! Give her the best treatment. I can afford it. Goodbye.'

When Andrew went upstairs, he found Mrs Lawrence waiting for him outside Toppy's room.

Every day Frances Lawrence was present at the time of his visit. Her quiet, gentle manner attracted Andrew. Although he did not realize it, she soon began to influence some of his actions.

She suggested that he should buy a car for his work. Andrew made no mention of this to Christine, but he began to ask himself how any doctor could develop a high-class practice without a car. A man in his position must not be seen walking down the street, carrying his own bag! He could not afford to buy a car in one payment; but he could spread out his payments over two or three years. Any garage would agree to that arrangement.

Three weeks later, Andrew drove home in an expensive new car. He ran into the house and called out: 'Christine! Christine! Come and see something!'

He had meant to surprise her, and he succeeded.

'*Andrew!* Is this ours? Oh, what a beauty!'

He smiled at her, 'Step inside, lady, and I'll take you for a drive!'

She admired the car again and again as he drove her through the streets. They went out together so rarely now that she made the most of every minute. She said happily: 'Now perhaps we can drive into the country on Sundays. Oh, that would be so nice!'

The suggestion annoyed Andrew. 'Oh, all right – I suppose so!' he answered. 'But we can't make a habit of driving into the country. The car is for work – not for pleasure.'

They drove home in silence.

On Thursday, as he was leaving the le Roys' house, Andrew

met Freddie Hamson. 'Hullo, Hamson,' he said.

Freddie looked at him in surprise. 'Why, hullo! What are you doing here?'

'Patient!' Andrew answered, pointing towards the house. 'I'm attending le Roy's daughter.'

'Le Roy!'

Delighted at Freddie's surprise, Andrew proudly put his hand on the door of his new car and asked: 'Which way are you going? Can I drive you anywhere?'

'I'm going to Ida Sherrington's Nursing Home,' said Freddie. 'You can drive me there, if you like.'

As they drove to the nursing home, both men were silent. Hamson was thinking. He had given Andrew a warm welcome when he came to London because he had hoped that Manson might occasionally ask for his opinion about a case, for which he would be able to charge the patient three pounds. But now this surprising change in his old friend – his new clothes, the car and his mention of le Roy – gave Hamson reason to believe that Andrew might be more helpful to him than he had expected.

'Come in and meet Ida,' he suggested when they reached the nursing home. 'Her home is one of the worst in London, but she makes a lot of money. She's a person worth knowing!'

'Yes?'

'Come in with me and see my patient – old Mrs Raeburn. Ivory and I are doing a few tests on her. Come and examine her chest. That would please her. And she'd pay you five pounds!'

'What! You mean . . .? But what's the matter with her chest?'

'Nothing!' Freddie smiled. 'Don't look so surprised! That's how we work here – Ivory, Deedman and I. You really ought to join up with us. The success of our system would surprise you.'

Andrew got out of the car and looked at the tall, cold building. He then turned his head and listened to the noise of the cars and the buses in the street. He asked himself how any sick person could find peace here. Andrew mentioned this to Hamson as they entered the building.

'Yes – it is noisy,' Freddie agreed. 'But the area is very convenient for us. That's all that matters.'

He led Andrew into a small office, where a fat woman with a red face sat at a desk.

'Good morning, Ida,' Freddie called out. 'I've brought Dr Manson to see you.'

Ida greeted Manson in a friendly manner. After they had talked together for a few minutes, Freddie interrupted them. 'Take a good look at him,' he said to Ida. 'He'll soon be sending you a lot of patients.'

Hamson laughed, and then led Andrew upstairs to see Mrs Raeburn. She was a woman of about sixty. Freddie sat on her bed and talked to her. He told her that Mr Ivory would call next day to tell her about the result of his important tests; and he asked her to allow Dr Manson, who had made a special study of lungs, to examine her chest. Mrs Raeburn was delighted at the suggestion. She enjoyed the examination. She was a rich woman and liked to spend her money on her health.

'Heavens!' Freddie said as they left the room. 'You've no idea how much money we have made from that old woman!'

Andrew did not answer. This place gave him a feeling of disgust. There was nothing wrong with the old lady, and Freddie's behaviour was shameful. He shook hands with Hamson and drove away.

At the end of the month, when he received a cheque for five pounds from Mrs Raeburn, he decided that he had been foolish to feel as he did. He had given her his services and had earned this payment! He accepted the cheque.

Chapter 27   Getting Rich

Andrew's hard times were over. So many people now came to his surgery that he could no longer take the time to give them proper attention.

'Listen, Chris,' he said one morning, 'I've just thought of an idea to save time. I want you to deal with the medicines for me. I usually spend about five minutes mixing each patient's medicine. During those five minutes I could examine another patient!'

She looked at him. 'But I don't know anything about medicine!'

He smiled. 'That doesn't matter, dear. I have prepared a large quantity of two different kinds of medicine. I will tell you which kind to give each patient. Then you will fill the bottle and hand it to him.'

Christine looked worried, 'But – oh, Andrew, do you really believe–'

'Oh, I know that I used to talk a lot of nonsense about medicine at Aberalaw! But I'm a practical doctor now. These medicines can't do any harm!'

Christine knew that it would be a waste of breath to argue with him; and so she agreed to fill the bottles. At every surgery, Andrew would run into her room to tell her which medicine to give each patient, and then run back to his surgery to attend to the next patient.

On one occasion, Christine told him that one of the medicines was finished. 'Never mind – give the other!' Andrew shouted. 'Give coloured water! Give anything!'

After the evening surgery, Andrew would sit down and work out his accounts. 'Heavens, Chris, we are doing well!' he said proudly one evening. 'Do you remember that miserable sum that I earned on our first day here? Well, today – today I made over eight pounds!' He locked up the money in a drawer, and praised his wisdom in buying the practice. 'Yes, and I'm attending high-class patients as well. We're going to be rich, woman!'

Soon, he was able to tell her to buy new furniture for the house. 'Go to the best shop. Get all the new furniture that you want. Get everything!'

Christine looked at him in silence.

He smiled. 'That's the joy of making money! One can buy everything that one wants. Let us enjoy our success!'

'By buying expensive furniture?'

He did not notice the bitterness in her voice. He laughed. 'That's right, dear. Now's the time to get rid of all those terrible old bits and pieces!'

She burst into tears. 'You weren't ashamed of it at Aberalaw. Oh, those were happy days!' She turned and ran out of the room.

Andrew was very surprised. He thought angrily; 'She doesn't care about my success – she doesn't care!'

But other people showed him respect.

A week after his quarrel with Christine, Mrs Lawrence telephoned and invited him to a lunch party on the following Friday. 'One or two important people who I would like you to meet will also be there,' she told him.

Feeling that he would be foolish to miss any opportunity of meeting people who might help him, Andrew accepted the invitation. But he did not want to run the risk of having another quarrel with Christine; and so, when Friday came, he told her that he was going to have lunch with Hamson. With a feeling of relief, he jumped into his car and drove to the home of Mrs Lawrence.

Several well-known people, including one of London's most famous doctors, were at the lunch party. The meal was excellent, with plenty of wine. Andrew drank, laughed, joined in the conversation, and enjoyed every moment. Although much of the conversation was as stupid as the talk at Hamson's party, Andrew returned home with a feeling of satisfaction.

But next morning he had a shock. Freddie telephoned him to inquire: 'Did you enjoy your lunch yesterday? How did I know about it? Haven't you seen the newspapers?'

Andrew ran to the sitting room, and hurriedly turned the pages of his newspaper. To his great surprise, he saw a photograph of Frances Lawrence and a report of her party, with the names of all the guests. He tore out the page and threw it into the fire.

But Christine had already read the newspaper. She felt deeply hurt. Why had he not told her? Why? Why? She felt more sorry for Andrew than for herself. She knew that rich people could be ill as well as poor people; but she felt that Andrew was giving up all his beliefs simply to make money.

Sadly, she attempted to do her housework.

Suddenly the telephone rang. As Andrew had by now gone out, she answered it. Her eyes became bright, excited. She kept looking out of the window, eager for Andrew's return. She forgot her sadness. She had received good news!

When Andrew returned, she ran into the hall and called out to him: 'Andrew! Sir Robert Abbey has just telephoned. Darling! You have been appointed to a post at the Victoria Hospital.'

Tears of excitement came to his eyes. 'Why – that's good news, Chris!'

'Isn't it? Isn't it?' she cried. She put her arms round his neck and kissed him.

He looked down at her, touched by her love. 'How good you are, Chris! And how bad I am!' he said.

Chapter 28   Denny Returns

To his great pride, Andrew was now a doctor in one of the oldest and most famous hospitals in London.

The Victoria was certainly old. The building was in a noisy, dirty street and it rarely saw the sun, even in summer. The department in which Andrew worked smelt of old age.

Andrew worked at the Victoria on two afternoons a week, and all his patients had some form of lung disease. But, though he was excited about his new appointment, Andrew could not put his heart into his work. He had lost interest in his coal dust discoveries. He had more important things to think about now! He decided that it was not worth his time and trouble to make a thorough medical examination of every person who came to see him. Instead, he took a quick look at each patient, and then gave him or her a bottle of medicine.

Six weeks after he started work at the Victoria, Andrew received a letter from Denny. He gave a sudden cry of pleasure. 'He's coming home – to work in England. Heavens, it will be nice to see him again, Chris!'

She was as pleased as Andrew was – but for a different reason. She had always felt that Denny and Hope had been a good influence on Andrew, and she hoped that Denny might influence his behaviour now. 'I think that I will invite Denny and Hope to dinner next week,' she said.

'All right,' he replied, 'but they will have to come on Sunday. I'm too busy during the rest of the week!'

On the following Sunday, Denny arrived. He looked older, but seemed to be happier. Yet he was the same Denny.

'This is a very grand house!' he greeted them. Then, turning to Christine, he added: 'And who is this well-dressed gentleman? Is he Dr Manson?'

Seated, a moment later, he refused a drink. 'No, thanks. I don't drink now. I'm going to settle down.'

He told them that he had found himself a good post at a country hospital.

Andrew looked at him quickly. 'You shouldn't bury yourself in the country, Philip! With your degree, you could get a much better post in London. Come to London!'

'What have you been doing to him?' Denny asked Christine. 'He doesn't sound like the man who blew up that sewer with me at Drineffy!'

At that moment Hope arrived. He and Denny had not met before; but they liked each other at once. Five minutes later, as they sat down to dinner, they began to joke about Andrew's success to his face.

'Of course, Hope,' Philip remarked sadly, 'I have known these people for a long time. I knew the Doctor before he came to London – before he became so successful! He was dismissed from his last post for using animals in his research!'

Hope laughed loudly and replied with another joke about Andrew.

There was more of this sort of talk during the meal. Then, as Christine had hoped, the conversation became more serious. At first, Andrew was rather quiet. Although he was pleased to see Philip again, he did not feel that his old friend was showing enough respect for his success. After all, he had done very well – extremely well! And what had Denny done? Several times he nearly told Denny and Hope to stop trying to be funny. Yet, when they began to discuss hospitals, Andrew joined in the conversation with real interest.

'They're all out of date!' he cried. 'The Victoria is falling down! Most of the hospitals in London are falling down! The buildings are old, and the streets are noisy! How can patients get well in such conditions? The whole system is wrong!'

'Well, what's the answer?' Philip asked, with an annoying

smile. 'What do you suggest? A new Board of Control, with you in charge, to reorganize all the hospitals?'

'Don't be a fool, Denny!' Andrew answered angrily. 'The only sensible answer is to build new hospitals a few kilometres outside London – in quiet areas, where there is good, fresh air. I tell you: the present system is terrible. And what are we doing about it? Nothing! If I were in charge . . .'

They talked until after midnight. Denny complained about the lack of knowledge shown by so many doctors; and Hope complained about the waste of medical supplies.

Soon after midnight, Hope left. While Andrew was out of the room, saying goodbye to him, Denny gave Christine a small present which he had brought home for her from abroad. She tried to thank him, but he stopped her. His kind eyes avoiding hers, Denny said: 'Don't worry about Andrew.' He smiled. 'But we must try to lead him back to his old Drineffy standards, mustn't we?'

Chapter 29　Money from Mr Ivory

Soon after Denny's visit, a Mrs Thornton requested Andrew to call and see her daughter, Sybil, who had hurt her foot. When Andrew examined her foot, he decided that the only way to cure the trouble was by a simple operation. 'I should have this done before the foot gets worse,' he advised Mrs Thornton.

'I will take your advice, Doctor,' she said. 'Will you make the arrangements for this, please? Who do you suggest does the operation?'

For a moment, Andrew could not think of anyone. Then suddenly he remembered Ivory. 'Mr Ivory might do this for us – if he's not too busy,' he said.

Andrew went home and telephoned Ivory, whose manner was

most friendly. He examined the girl, and agreed that an operation was necessary; and two days later, he did the operation in Miss Sherrington's Nursing Home.

Andrew was present, because Ivory said that it was important for him to be present. Two weeks later, when Sybil Thornton had left the nursing home, Ivory invited him to lunch. During the meal, he suggested to Andrew: 'Leave the money arrangements for the operation to me. I hear that the Thorntons are very rich. I can charge them more than you can.' He paused. 'Er, there is another matter that I ought to mention: Sybil's tonsils are in a bad state. Did you examine them?'

'No – no, I didn't.'

'Oh, they're very bad! I hope you don't mind, but I told Mrs Thornton that we would take out Sybil's tonsils as soon as the weather is warm.'

On his way home, Andrew thought: 'What a pleasant man Ivory is – so nice and easy to work with!'

About a month later, while he was having tea with Christine, the afternoon post brought him a friendly letter from Ivory, enclosing a cheque for twenty pounds. Andrew looked at the cheque in surprise. He had done nothing to help Ivory at the operation! With a smile, he handed the letter and cheque to Christine. 'This is very generous, isn't it, Chris?'

She looked confused. 'But I don't understand. Is this in payment of your bill to Mrs Thornton?'

He laughed. 'No, no! This is an additional payment – for the time that I spent at the operation. I earned this just for being there.'

She put the cheque on the table. 'It seems a lot of money for doing nothing!'

'Well, why not? The Thorntons are very rich. They can easily afford it!'

When Andrew had gone, Christine looked at the cheque again.

She had not realized that he was working with Ivory. Suddenly all her worries returned. How fond of money he had become! Money seemed to be the only thing that mattered to him! Tears came to her eyes. She must speak to him.

That evening, after surgery, she asked slowly: 'Andrew, will you do something to please me? Will you drive me into the country on Sunday?'

He looked at her strangely. 'Well – oh, all right!'

On Sunday, a fine spring day, they drove to a village a few miles from London, where they ate their lunch – which they had brought with them – by some woods.

As they sat in the sunshine, Christine took a deep breath. 'Andrew, dear,' she said. 'I want to speak to you. Money isn't the only thing in life! Please listen to me. Please! You have changed so much, Andrew! Denny noticed the difference in you, too! You're not the Andrew Manson that I married! Oh, if only you could be as you used to be!'

'What have I done wrong now?' Andrew shouted.

'It's your whole behaviour, love! That cheque that Ivory sent you – it's not right to accept it!'

He stiffened. 'Not right! Why shouldn't I accept it?'

'Oh, can't you understand what I mean? You're doing all the things that used to make you so angry with other doctors! Oh, Andrew, don't lose all respect for yourself.' She suddenly burst into tears.

He looked at her in anger. 'Oh, stop crying, you fool! Try to help me, instead of complaining every minute of the day! You talk as if I were a criminal. I only want to succeed. Don't mention this nonsense to me again.'

'All right,' she cried. 'I won't. But I warn you: one day you will be sorry.'

They hardly spoke to each other for the rest of the day.

Towards the end of the week, Andrew went to tea with Mrs

Lawrence, who always seemed to approve of his actions.

'Why,' suggested Mrs Lawrence, 'don't you rent a room in this part of London for this high-class practice that you are so anxious to develop? Many more people with money would come to you if you had a room in this area.'

Half an hour later, as Andrew drove home, he thought about Mrs Lawrence's suggestion. It was a good idea! Without saying anything to Christine, he began to search for a room in the West End of London. When he found one, about a month later, he told her at breakfast: 'It may interest you to know that I have rented a room in Welbeck Street. I shall use the surgery here for people who have not much money, and my new room in the West End for my rich patients.'

Chapter 30   Lunch with Mr Stillman

The room in Welbeck Street gave Andrew a new feeling of his own importance. Frances Lawrence and Freddie Hamson made suggestions about decorations and furniture; and Hamson also found him a nurse – Nurse Sharp, a rather bitter but hard-working woman, who was a friend of the nurse that Freddie employed.

When his room was ready, it looked very grand. Andrew decided that he could charge his patients at least three pounds a visit here.

For the first week or two very few people came to see him, but then patients began to flood in. He was a busy man, driving backwards and forwards in his expensive car from his home to his Welbeck Street office, and from there to the Victoria Hospital. He rarely finished work until ten o'clock at night.

In June Ivory took out Sybil Thornton's tonsils, and posted Andrew a cheque in payment for attending the operation.

One afternoon soon after this an old woman called to see Andrew about her throat. Her condition was quite easy to cure, but Andrew decided to send her to Hamson for his advice about the best treatment to give: Freddie had been so kind of late that he wanted to give him this opportunity to earn himself an easy three pounds. A week or two later Hamson, in return, sent Andrew one of his patients to examine.

That evening, as he drove home from his West End consulting room, Andrew felt very pleased with himself. But he found Christine far from pleased.

'Mrs Lawrence telephoned you again this afternoon. No message!' she told him.

He turned red. 'What do you mean – again?'

'This is the fourth time that she has telephoned you this week!'

'Well?'

'Nothing! I didn't say anything.'

'It's how you look. It's not my fault if she telephones me!'

He rushed out of the room. At once he felt sorry. Relations between Christine and himself were getting worse – and they had once been so happy! He had a sudden desire to please her. The next minute, he was in his car, driving to see Miss Cramb at her shop.

When he returned, he went into the living room and called out: 'Christine! Come here a moment!'

She came at once.

'Look, dear!' Andrew said awkwardly. 'I've bought you this. I know – I know that we have been quarrelling of late. But this ought to show you–' He broke off, and handed her a box.

As she opened it, her hands trembled. Then she gave a little cry. 'What a lovely, lovely dress!' Tears were running down her face. She turned to him excitedly. 'You do love me, don't you, dear? That's all that matters to me.'

He smiled. 'Of course I do. Listen, Chris – I'll take you out to dinner today.'

He took her to a very expensive restaurant. 'We didn't have this sort of food in Drineffy!' he laughed, as they began their meal.

Andrew was determined to have a good time; but Christine could not be cheerful. The room was crowded, hot and noisy. The noise of these rich people was hateful to her. Suddenly, she felt sick.

'What's the matter?' Andrew asked. 'Aren't you enjoying yourself?'

'Yes, of course.' She tried to smile.

'You haven't listened to a word that I've been saying! You haven't drunk any of your wine! When a man takes his wife out–'

'Can I have a little water?' she asked weakly. She wanted to shout. She hated the place!

They finished their meal in silence, and drove home. Their relations were even worse than before. Christine felt terribly miserable. She began to lose her self-confidence; to ask herself if she was really the right wife for Andrew.

But Andrew's worries at home were pushed into the background when, next day, he read in a newspaper that Richard Stillman – the man with a hospital in America who had written to praise his coal dust experiments – had come to England and was staying at a hotel in London.

Stillman had no medical qualifications. After leaving school, he had begun to study medicine at an American university; but before he had finished his studies his father died, leaving his mother very little money. In order to support his mother and sister, Stillman left the university to earn his living in an old family business. He hated this work. He continued to study medicine in his free time and, when he had saved enough money, he returned to the medical profession. But so many valuable years had been wasted that Stillman did not take a degree. Instead, he built a hospital for the treatment of people with lung diseases. At first, the American doctors refused to recognize him. But Stillman cured so many people that other doctors had failed to cure that he gradually won the respect of the American medical profession.

The English doctors still refused to recognize Stillman, but Andrew felt the greatest respect for him. He wrote to him at once, inviting him to lunch at the expensive restaurant to which he had taken Christine.

Next morning, Stillman telephoned him. 'Dr Manson,' he said. 'I should like to meet you for lunch – but not at that restaurant. I hate the place! Come and have lunch at my hotel.'

When they had taken their seats at a quiet table in the dining room of his hotel, Stillman gave Andrew a friendly smile and said: 'It's very nice to be in England. I like your country.'

'What is the reason for your visit?' Andrew asked.

Stillman smiled. 'As a matter of fact, I have come to England to start a small hospital – like my hospital in America. I am building it in the lovely Chiltern Hills, to the north-west of London. I expect that you know the area.'

Andrew leaned forward. 'That's interesting! I should like to see your hospital.'

'I shall be delighted to show you round as soon as the place is ready. We shall treat mainly chest diseases, and I have one or two new ideas that may interest you.'

'Really? Tell me about them.'

They spent most of the afternoon discussing Stillman's new hospital.

Andrew left Stillman with a strange feeling of excitement. But when he returned home, he found Christine reading a prayer book; for some reason that he could not explain, this annoyed him. 'Good heavens!' he shouted. 'Have you nothing better to do?'

'What's wrong? I used to read my prayer book before I met you.'

'Oh, did you? Well, let me tell you this: you're a fool!'

'Perhaps. But I would prefer to be a fool and keep my self-respect than to be successful with no self-respect!' With a great effort, she kept back her tears. Then, in a quiet voice, she said: 'Andrew, don't you think that it would be a good idea if I went away for a short time? Mrs Vaughan has invited me to stay with her for two or three weeks. Don't you think that I ought to go?'

'Yes! Go! Go at once!' He turned and left the room.

Chapter 31   Mary Boland

Christine's absence was at first a relief to Andrew. Then he began to ask himself what she was doing, and to look forward to her return. Although he told himself that he was now a free man, he had the same lonely feeling that he had experienced at Aberalaw when Christine had gone away to stay with her aunt.

He met Ivory, Freddie and Deedman two or three times. He also drove to the Chiltern Hills to see Stillman's new hospital. He and Stillman became good friends. But his friendship with Stillman did not take away his loneliness.

In the end, Andrew telephoned Frances Lawrence and asked her: 'Would you care to drive into the country and have dinner with me tomorrow evening?'

Her voice comforted him. 'That would be very nice.'

The next evening they drove to a small country town, where they had dinner at a hotel by the river.

'We have known each other for quite a long time,' Frances remarked, 'but this is the first occasion that you have asked me to come out with you.'

'Are you sorry that you came?'

She smiled.

'Does – does your husband know that we . . .'

She looked up. 'Don't you understand? Jack and I are good friends. But we . . .' She stopped suddenly. 'Let's dance,' she suggested.

They danced. It gave Andrew a strange feeling of pleasure to hold her in his arms. When they returned to their table, he asked awkwardly: 'Why have you been so kind to me?'

His question seemed to amuse her. 'You are very attractive. And what I like most about you is that you do not realize it!'

'No – do be serious!'

She laughed. 'It's hot in here! Let's go outside and look at the moonlight on the river.'

They walked down to the river and sat on a seat. She looked at the moon shining on the water. 'What a beautiful night!' she said.

He kissed her. Her lips were warm.

She smiled. 'That was very sweet – but very badly done!'

'I can do better,' he whispered. He felt awkward, ashamed. He wanted to take her into his arms. But then a shadowy picture of Christine's tired, sad face looked up at him from the water. It worried and annoyed him. He kissed Frances again.

'You took a long time to do that!' she said. 'And now, Doctor, I think that we should go home.'

They drove back to London in silence. Andrew was not happy. He hated himself. He tried to dismiss Christine from his mind but he could not do so. When they reached Mrs Lawrence's house, he got out of the car and opened the door for her without a word.

'Come in,' she invited him.

He paused. 'It's very late, isn't it?'

She went indoors without answering. And he followed her.

Three days later, Andrew sat in his West End office, feeling tired and miserable.

Suddenly Nurse Sharp entered. 'There's a man to see you – a Mr Boland. I've told him he'll have to wait.'

'Boland?' Andrew repeated tiredly, as if he had never heard the name before. Then suddenly his face brightened. 'Con Boland? Show him in, Nurse! At once!'

'But a patient is waiting to see you.'

'Never mind about that!' he shouted. 'Do what I say!'

Nurse Sharp, annoyed at being addressed in that manner, gave Andrew one look and went out of the room. A minute later, she showed Boland in.

'Why, Con!' Andrew called out, jumping up from his chair.

'Hullo! Hullo!' shouted Con, walking quickly forward to shake hands with Andrew. 'Heavens, Manson, it's nice to see you again! You're looking well! Well, well, this is a high-class practice!' He looked at Nurse Sharp, who was watching him with scorn. 'This nurse of yours refused to admit me at first!'

Nurse Sharp turned and walked out of the room.

After she had left, Con's manner changed. 'Listen, Manson,' he said, 'I've come to see you about my daughter Mary. She's ill. Llewellyn has been attending her, but – well, he's useless.' Con suddenly became angry. 'He says that Mary has tuberculosis and cannot be cured. Listen, Manson, will you do something for me? I know that you're a successful doctor now, but – will you examine Mary? I have such confidence in you – and so has Mary.'

Andrew was worried. 'Mary – poor girl! I'll do everything that I can for her – everything,' he promised Con.

At that moment, Nurse Sharp entered. 'Five patients are waiting to see you now, Dr Manson,' she informed him.

Andrew took no notice, but continued to talk to Con. He

invited Boland to stay with him for a few days, and Boland accepted his invitation joyfully.

Con's cheerful spirit helped him to forget his troubles with Christine. When she returned on Friday, Andrew took Con with him to the railway station to meet her. He was afraid to meet Christine by himself, after all that had happened, and he hoped that Con's presence might make things easier for both of them.

'Hullo, Chris!' Andrew called out cheerfully as she got out of the train. 'Look who's here! Con! He's staying with us, Chris! Did you enjoy yourself?'

Christine was surprised at her warm welcome. She had feared that she might not be met at all! Sitting in the back seat of the car with Con, she talked excitedly.

'Oh, I am glad to be home again!' she said when they reached the house. She took a deep breath. 'Have you missed me, Andrew?'

'Missed you? I most certainly have.'

After a few minutes Andrew, who still felt awkward, said that he must visit a patient and hurriedly left the house. 'Thank heavens that's over!' he said to himself as he got into his car. 'I'm sure that she has no suspicions about Frances. That's all that matters at the moment.'

While he was out, Con had a long talk with Christine about Mary's health. Christine felt very anxious, and advised Con to telephone Mary, telling her to come to London at once.

When Mary arrived next day, her thin face and body gave Andrew a shock. He ordered her to bed, and examined her chest. Fifteen minutes later, he returned to the living room looking very worried.

'I'm afraid, Con, that Llewellyn was right. Mary has got tuberculosis,' he told him. 'But don't worry. The disease is in the early stage of development.'

'You mean that she can be cured?'

'Yes. But she must go into hospital for special treatment. There is a doctor at the Victoria Hospital, Dr Thoroughgood, who has made a special study of this disease. I will ask him to treat her. And, if she comes into my hospital, I can watch her progress.'

'Manson, you're a true friend!' said Con.

On Saturday afternoon Mary was admitted to the Victoria Hospital, and Con returned to Aberalaw.

'How nice to be together again, Chris!' Andrew said, after he had left.

He sounded sincere. But, for some reason, Christine did not believe that he really meant what he said. She went upstairs to her bedroom and cried to herself: 'Oh God, when and how will this end?'

Chapter 32 Harry Vidler's Operation

Andrew's dreams of success and wealth were coming true. His practice was growing every week. His business relations with Hamson and Ivory were very close, and were earning him a lot of money. Deedman was also sending him patients. And now le Roy, who owned a large food factory, had offered him a post as medical adviser to his company. Andrew had a feeling of power; he could do nothing wrong.

Then – quite suddenly and without warning – his whole life was changed.

One evening in November the wife of a shoemaker came to his house. Her name was Mrs Vidler, a small, cheerful woman of middle age whom Andrew knew well.

'Doctor,' she said, 'my husband is ill. He has been ill for several weeks, but he refused to come to you because he didn't want to trouble you. Will you call and see him, Doctor?'

When Andrew called next morning, Harry Vidler was in bed with a bad pain in his stomach. He examined Vidler and found that, although not seriously ill, he needed an operation to be done quickly. He explained this to the Vidlers, who asked him to arrange for a good surgeon to do the operation in a nursing home.

That evening Andrew telephoned Ivory. 'I would like you to do a stomach operation, Ivory,' he said. 'The patient is a shoemaker. He has very little money; and so I shall be grateful if you will reduce your charges for him.'

Ivory was pleasant. They discussed the case for several minutes; and then Andrew telephoned Mrs Vidler.

'Mr Ivory, a West End surgeon, has agreed to do this operation for thirty pounds,' he told her. 'His usual charge is a hundred pounds. So I think this is very satisfactory.'

'Yes, Doctor, yes.' She sounded worried. 'It's very kind of you to arrange this for us. We'll find the money somehow.'

A few days later, Ivory did the operation in a private nursing home. Vidler was very cheerful. Before he was put to sleep, he smiled at Andrew and said: 'I shall feel better after this.' The next moment he was asleep.

Ivory took his surgeon's knife and made a long cut in Vidler's stomach. At once a large flesh bag of poisonous matter sprang out of the wound like a wet ball. This bag was the cause of Vidler's pain. Ivory tried to catch hold of the ball and cut it away from the inside of the stomach. He must have tried 20 times, but on each attempt the ball slipped out of his hand.

Andrew looked at Ivory in annoyance, thinking: 'What is the man doing? Why does he find it so difficult?' Suddenly he realized that this was the first stomach operation that Ivory had done for him. He walked nearer to the table. Nobody else seemed to be worried. Ivory, the doctor who had put Vidler to sleep, and the nurses were all quite calm. But for some reason,

Andrew had a feeling of fear.

In the end, Ivory gave up the attempt, and cut a hole in the bag itself. At once the bag burst, and spilled the poisonous matter into the stomach wound.

Andrew watched in disgust. But still Ivory was not worried. He cleaned away some of the poison, and then tried, without success, to stop the bleeding. A wave of anger swept over Andrew. 'Good heavens,' he thought, 'this man is not a surgeon! He has no idea what he is doing.'

The second doctor said in a quiet voice: 'I'm afraid that he's dying, Ivory.'

Ivory did not answer, did not appear to hear.

'Yes – he's dead now,' said the other doctor.

Ivory laid down his instruments. 'A pity!' he remarked. 'The shock of the operation must have killed him.'

Andrew could not speak. He suddenly remembered Mrs Vidler, who was waiting downstairs.

Ivory read his thoughts. 'Don't worry, Manson,' he said, 'I'll speak to the little woman for you. Come with me.'

Andrew followed him down the stairs to the room where Mrs Vidler was waiting.

'My dear lady,' said Ivory, putting his hand gently on her shoulder, 'I'm afraid that we have bad news for you. Your poor husband, in spite of everything that we did for him–'

She turned white. 'Harry!' she whispered.

'Nobody,' Ivory continued, sadly, 'could have saved him. And even if he had lived–'

She looked up at him. 'I understand. Thank you, Doctor, for being so kind.' She began to cry.

He went out of the room, and again Andrew followed him.

'Well, that's done!' Ivory said coldly. 'I'm sorry, Manson. I didn't expect that to happen. Of course, the man didn't die during the operation. I had finished before he died. So there is nothing to worry about. There'll be no need for an inquiry.'

Andrew was trembling with anger. 'Oh, stop talking!' he shouted. 'You killed him! You're not a surgeon! You never were and you never will be a surgeon!'

Ivory gave Andrew a bitter look. 'I advise you not to talk in that manner, Manson!'

'It's the truth! Oh, God, why did I trust you? Why?'

'Be silent, you fool!'

Andrew was almost blind with anger. 'You know that it's the truth. You did the operation so badly that it was almost murder!'

For a moment it seemed as if Ivory would hit him. But, with a great effort, he controlled himself, and walked out of the room.

With a sad heart and an aching head, Andrew went home. He returned just in time for his evening surgery. Many people were waiting to see him. He looked at them and thought: 'The same stupid faces! There's nothing wrong with most of them!'

He then went into his room and began his duties. Trying to behave in his usual friendly manner, Andrew made polite conversation with each patient, and then told Christine which medicine to give him. After the surgery, he sat down to work out his accounts, as was his custom every evening. But he could not think clearly.

'Well, how much money have you made today?' Christine asked him.

He did not, could not, answer. When she left the room, he sat quite still, like a man in a dream. 'Oh, God, what have I done? What have I done?' he kept saying. Suddenly he noticed the bag of money which his patients had paid him for his services that day. Another wave of anger swept over him. He picked up the bag and threw it across the room.

He jumped up from his chair. He was hot; he could hardly breathe. He ran outside to the back of the house, and was sick.

Chapter 33   A Change of Heart

Andrew could not sleep that night. Next morning he felt half dead. He ate no breakfast, but just drank one cup of coffee.

His first thought now was for Mary Boland. He got out his car, and drove straight to the Victoria Hospital to see how she was.

'Good morning,' she said, when he entered her room. 'Aren't my flowers beautiful? Christine brought them yesterday.'

He sat on her bed and looked at her. She seemed to be thinner! 'Yes, they are nice flowers. How do you feel, Mary?'

'Oh – all right.' Her eyes avoided his. 'Anyway, you'll soon make me better!'

Her confidence in him added to his misery. He thought: 'If any harm comes to Mary, I will never forgive myself.'

At that moment, Dr Thoroughgood entered. 'Good morning, Manson,' he said pleasantly. 'Why, what's the matter with you? Are you ill?'

Andrew stood up. 'I'm quite well, thank you.'

Dr Thoroughgood gave him a strange look, and then turned to Mary. They examined Mary together, and then walked over to a corner of the room, where they could not be heard, and discussed her case.

'It seems to me,' said Andrew, 'that her progress is not at all satisfactory.'

Dr Thoroughgood rubbed his hands. 'Oh, I don't know, Manson.'

'Her temperature is higher.'

'Yes. But–'

'This case is very important to me. I don't want to tell you your business but I think that you should do an operation on her lung. I suggested this when Mary first came into hospital.'

Thoroughgood was annoyed. 'I don't agree with you,' he said. 'I'm sorry, Manson, but you must allow me to treat this case in the way that I consider best.'

Andrew felt too weak to argue. He went back to Mary, told her that he would call to see her again on the following day, and left the hospital.

It was now nearly one o'clock. He went to a cheap restaurant, where he drank another cup of coffee but ate no food, and then drove to his office in Welbeck Street, where Nurse Sharp, who was in a bad temper, also inquired if he felt ill.

His first patient was a young man with a weak heart. Andrew gave him a thorough examination, and then asked him many questions before deciding on the treatment to give him. When, at the end of the examination, the young man tried to pay him for his services, Andrew said quickly: 'Please don't pay me now. Wait till I send you a bill.' The thought that he would never send a bill, that he had lost his desire for money and now hated it, comforted him strangely.

His second patient was a rich woman of forty-five, Miss Basden, who visited him every few days. Smiling sweetly, she began to tell him about her imaginary aches and pains.

Andrew interrupted her. 'Why do you come to me, Miss Basden?'

She stopped in the middle of a sentence and looked at him in surprise.

'Oh, I know – I'm to blame,' he said. 'I told you to come. But there's nothing the matter with you.'

'Dr Manson!'

'I'm sorry,' he said. 'I can be of no further service to you, Miss Basden. But I am sure that there are many other doctors in this area who will be very pleased to tell you that you are ill, and to give you expensive treatments.'

She opened her mouth to speak, but no words came. Then she hurried out of the room.

Andrew was about to go home, when Nurse Sharp came in

smiling. 'Dr Hamson to see you!'

The next minute Freddie entered. His manner had never been so friendly. 'Listen, Manson,' he said. 'I have heard about that operation yesterday, and I think that you were quite right to be angry with Ivory. It was shameful! As a matter of fact, old man, I'm rather annoyed with Ivory and Deedman. We've been working together – sending each other patients – but they haven't been paying me my fair share of the money. They're cheats! I could tell you a lot of other things about them, too!' Hamson paused. 'Listen, old man, I've got an idea! Let's work together – you and I – without Ivory and Deedman. We don't need them! I know all the tricks – all the ways to make money. And you're a clever doctor. If we work together, we'll make a fortune!'

Andrew sat quite still. He felt no anger against Hamson, only a bitter hatred of himself. At last, he said: 'I'm sorry: I can't work with you, Freddie. I'm tired of all this! There are too many doctors whose only thought is to make money.'

Hamson's face turned red. 'What the—' He jumped up. 'Have you gone mad?'

'Perhaps. But I am going to stop thinking about money and success. A doctor shouldn't try to make money out of sick people.'

'You're a fool!' shouted Hamson. He turned and rushed out of the room.

Andrew got up and drove home.

Christine was in the living room. The sight of her pale, sad face made him tremble. She said: 'You've had a busy day. Will you have some tea before the surgery?'

'There will be no surgery this evening,' he said.

She looked at him in surprise. 'But it's Saturday – your busiest night!'

He did not answer.

'Why, what is the matter?' she asked.

Andrew gave her one look. 'Christine!' he said. He ran forward and knelt at her feet, crying.

Chapter 34   A Visit to Mr Stillman

Next morning, which was Sunday, Andrew lay in bed beside Christine, talking and pouring out his feelings to her in the way that he used to do.

'Why did I do it? Was I crazy, Chris? Oh, Chris. I'm sorry!'

She smiled, actually smiled.

'Well,' Andrew continued. 'We must leave here now – sell the practice. Oh, Chris, I've thought of an excellent idea.'

'Yes, dear? What is it?'

'To join up with Denny and Hope! Each of us has special knowledge of a different branch of medicine. So we could do work of great value together – honest work, not simply making money. Denny and I have always said that a doctor who works alone attempts too much. I mean – he may know a lot about one subject but very little about another. Now, if we three work together, we can share our knowledge and provide a really useful medical service for our patients. Denny is a surgeon and can do the operations; I can do the general work of the practice; and Hope can do the scientific tests and give us advice on our problems.'

Christine looked at him with shining eyes. 'Oh, it's so nice to hear you talk like this! Oh, I'm so happy!'

'I believe that Denny and Hope will join with me,' Andrew said excitedly.

He jumped out of bed and began to walk up and down the room. Suddenly he stopped. 'Chris,' he said, 'there's something that I must do immediately. I'm very worried about Mary Boland. She's making no progress at the Victoria. Thoroughgood doesn't understand her case. I want to take Mary away from the Victoria and send her to Stillman's new hospital!'

'Stillman's?'

'Yes. It's the best hospital that I have ever seen. I intend to drive over and see Stillman today and try to persuade him to admit Mary! Will you come with me?'

'We'll leave as soon as you are ready!' she said.

When he had dressed, Andrew went downstairs and wrote long letters to Denny and Hope. Then, after a light meal, he and Christine drove to the Chiltern Hills. It was a long time since they had been so happy together.

They reached the hospital at three o'clock. Stillman gave them a warm welcome and showed them round his hospital, which, though small, was comfortable and full of modern equipment.

After this, they had tea with Stillman; and Andrew made his request. 'I want to ask you something, Mr Stillman,' he said quickly. 'Will you take over a case for me? A girl with tuberculosis – in its early stages. She's the daughter of a friend of mine, and she's making no progress at the Victoria Hospital.'

Stillman smiled. 'Surely you don't want to send *me* a case! English doctors don't recognize me! Remember that I have no medical qualifications! I cannot be trusted! I am more likely to kill than to cure!'

Andrew did not smile. 'Please don't joke, Mr Stillman. I'm serious! I'm very worried about this girl.'

'I'm afraid that I have no bed for her, my friend. I have a list of women who are already waiting to be admitted. Although the doctors don't like me, some people–'

'But, Mr Stillman,' Andrew interrupted, 'I was depending on you. If you don't admit Mary, she will never get well where she is.'

Stillman leaned forward and helped himself to a piece of cake. 'I see that you really are worried. All right, I will help you,' he promised. 'Bring Mary here next Wednesday and I will find her a bed. I will do my best to cure her.'

Andrew's face brightened. 'I – I can't thank you enough!'

'Then don't try to!' said Stillman.

Chapter 35   Mary Goes to Mr Stillman

Next morning Andrew rose early, after a good night's sleep. He felt excited, ready for anything. He went straight to the telephone and gave orders to a medical property firm to sell his practice. 'Sell it for a fair price. I won't accept any more than it's really worth,' he said. 'The people in this area have not got much money; and the next doctor may not do as well as I have done.'

At lunchtime Christine handed Andrew two letters. They were replies to his letters to Denny and Hope. The short note from Denny read: 'Interested. Expect me tomorrow evening.' The letter from Hope also expressed interest, though the words showed Hope's usual sense of fun.

After lunch, Andrew drove to the Victoria Hospital to see Mary Boland.

Sitting beside Mary's bed, he told her about the new arrangements that he had made. 'You'll like the other hospital better, Mary – much better,' he promised her. 'Now, I don't want to make difficulties here. So I would like you to pretend that it is your own wish to leave – say that you want to go home. Then, on Wednesday, I will pick you up and drive you to Stillman's hospital.'

Andrew returned home with a feeling that he was beginning to correct his mistakes. That evening, in his surgery, he sorted out the patients who really were ill from those who only imagined that they were. Again and again, he said firmly: 'This must be your last visit. You're better now. It won't do you any good to go on taking medicine!'

It was surprising how much comfort this gave him. After the surgery, he went in to Christine feeling several years younger.

At that moment the telephone rang. Christine went to answer it. When she returned, she looked worried again. 'Someone wants to speak to you,' she told him.

'Who?' Suddenly he realized that it was Frances Lawrence. 'Tell her that I've gone out,' he said. 'No – don't say that!' He walked quickly forward. 'I'll speak to her myself.'

He came back in five minutes and said: 'That's over, too! I shan't see *her* again!'

Christine smiled happily without answering.

On the following evening Denny came to dinner. He brought a message from Hope, saying he was sorry that he had another appointment. 'He said that he had work to do,' Denny remarked, knocking out his pipe. 'But I believe that his appointment is really with a young lady. I wouldn't be surprised if our friend Hope decides to marry her.'

'Did he say anything about my idea?' Andrew asked quickly.

'Yes – he's interested. And so am I. I am surprised that a man with your dull brains has the ability to think of such an excellent plan! Tell me about it.'

Andrew explained his plan with rising excitement. They then began to discuss the practical details.

'In my opinion,' said Denny, 'we ought to choose a town with a population of about 20,000 people – an industrial town where four or five doctors are all working against each other. In such a town, we would have the best opportunity to show the advantage of doctors with different medical qualifications working together. We might make enemies at first, but we would succeed in the end. Perhaps, after a time, we might start

107

our own hospital. Yes, this is a good idea.' Suddenly feeling Christine's eye on him, Denny smiled. 'And what do you think about it, Christine? Crazy, isn't it?'

'Yes,' she answered. 'But sometimes the crazy things are best!'

'You're right, Chris!' Andrew cried, hitting the table with his hand. 'Our aim must be to set an example in medical practice!'

They talked until such a late hour that Denny missed the last train home and had to spend the night with Andrew and Christine.

On the following Wednesday – by which time a Dr Lowry was on the point of buying his practice – Andrew went to the Victoria Hospital to take Mary Boland away. Everything had worked out just as he had planned. No objection was raised to Mary's leaving the Victoria, and at two o'clock Andrew arrived with Nurse Sharp to pick her up.

Nurse Sharp was in a bad temper because Andrew had just told her that he intended to close his office in Welbeck Street and had given her a month's notice. She sat with Mary in the back seat of the car and did not speak a single word during the journey.

They reached Stillman's hospital at half past three. As soon as Mary was in bed, Stillman went to her room to examine her. When he and Andrew entered the room, Nurse Sharp seemed surprised and annoyed. Stillman examined Mary very thoroughly, and then led Andrew out of the room again.

'She is very ill,' he said. 'I must do an operation on her lung immediately. It should have been done several weeks ago!'

While Stillman got ready for the operation, Andrew went back and told Mary of their decision. 'It's nothing to worry about, Mary,' Andrew comforted her. 'You won't feel any pain. I'll be in the room. I'll see that you're all right.'

Ten minutes later, Stillman began the operation. He worked

quickly and with great skill, employing several new ideas that he had discovered in America. Andrew had never witnessed a more skilful operation.

When it was over, and Mary was back in her bed, Andrew went in to see her. 'Well, do you feel happier now?'

She smiled. 'You were right – it was nothing to worry about!'

'All that you need now is rest. You'll soon be well again – completely cured!' he promised her.

Chapter 36   The Cheese from Mrs Smith

It was nearly seven o'clock when Andrew left Stillman's hospital. He now had peace of mind about Mary. Andrew realized that other doctors might question his action in sending Mary to Stillman. But he did not mind. He had done the best thing for the girl, and that was all that mattered.

He drove slowly, enjoying the quiet of the evening. Nurse Sharp again sat in the back of the car, without speaking. When they arrived back in London, he drove her to the place where she wished to get out and then went home.

Christine met him joyfully in the hall. Her eyes were shining. 'Sold!' she cried. 'Dr Lowry has bought the practice!'

He followed Christine into the living room, where the remains of her evening meal were on the table.

'Isn't it good news?' Christine continued. 'And we've sold it so quickly! I've been thinking! Let's go away for a holiday! We had such a lovely time–' She broke off suddenly. 'Why, what's the matter, dear? You look so strange!'

He smiled, and sat down. 'I suddenly feel a little tired – perhaps because I have had no dinner.'

'What!' she cried. 'I imagined that Mr Stillman had given you dinner.' She looked at the table. 'I've had mine!'

'It doesn't matter!'

'But it does matter! Wait there, and I'll get you some food. Would you like some soup – or an egg – or what?'

He thought. 'An egg, please, Chris. And perhaps a bit of cheese after that.'

Christine ran off and got him his meal. While he ate, she sat beside him talking excitedly about the future – about Andrew's plans to work with Denny and Hope. 'You know, dear,' she said. 'I feel as if we were starting a new life – the sort of life that we used to live! Oh, I'm so happy.'

He looked towards her. 'Are you really happy, Chris?'

She kissed him. 'I've never been happier in my life than I am at this moment.'

There was a pause. Andrew spread some butter on a piece of bread, and then lifted the lid of a dish to help himself to cheese. But the dish was empty.

At once Christine gave a little cry of shame. 'Oh, I meant to buy some more cheese from Mrs Smith today!'

'Oh, it's all right, Chris.'

'But it isn't all right! I'm a bad wife!' She jumped up, her eye on the clock. 'I'll run along to Mrs Smith now – before she closes her shop.'

'Oh, don't trouble, Chris, I–'

'Please, love!' She silenced him cheerfully. 'I *want* to do it. I want to because you love Mrs Smith's cheese – and I love *you*.'

She left the room before he could say another word. He heard her quick step in the hall, followed by the sound of the front door opening and closing. Smiling to himself, he sat back in his chair and waited for her return.

She was away for so long that he began to lose his hunger. 'I shan't want the cheese if she doesn't hurry up! She must be talking to Mrs Smith,' he thought.

Suddenly the doorbell rang violently. He looked up in surprise, and went into the hall. The bell rang again, more violently. He opened the front door.

A crowd of people stood in the darkness outside the house.

A policeman whom he knew well came forward, breathing heavily. 'Doctor, there's been an accident! Your wife ran – Oh, God! She ran across the street; and a bus . . .'

Icy fingers seemed to seize Andrew's heart. Before he could speak, the hall filled with people – Mrs Smith, who was in tears; the driver of the bus; another policeman, and two or three people who had witnessed the accident.

Then two men carried in his Christine. In her hand was the packet of cheese which she had just bought from Mrs Smith. They laid her on the bed in his surgery.

Chapter 37 Plans for the Future

Andrew broke down. For several days, he hardly knew what he was doing. Denny spent several hours with him each day, but Andrew did not seem to know he was there.

He went to Christine's funeral with Denny, and then spent the rest of the day drinking. Walking from room to room with an unsteady step, he shouted at himself: 'You're to blame for her death! This is a punishment for your crimes! You tried to make money; and that was a crime. Now God is punishing you!'

He crept upstairs, paused, and then went into Christine's bedroom. It was silent, cold and empty. On a table lay her handbag. He picked it up, held it against his face, and then, with a trembling hand, opened it. Inside, he found an old photograph of himself and the little notes that his grateful patients at Aberalaw had sent him with their Christmas presents. She had kept them for all those years! He fell on to his knees by the bed and cried.

Denny did not attempt to stop him from drinking. As Dr Lowry was already attending to the practice, and there was therefore no need for Andrew to work, Denny thought it wise to leave him alone for the moment. But after about a week Denny took action. 'We're going away,' he said simply.

Andrew did not argue, did not even ask where they were going. In silence, he watched Denny pack a bag for him. An hour later they were in the train, travelling to Wales.

They went to stay at a lonely village by a beautiful river in the mountains.

'I used to come here to fish. I think that this place should suit us,' said Denny, when they arrived at their small but comfortable hotel.

The next morning, Denny took Andrew for a walk. It was a nice fine day but Andrew, tired after a sleepless night, wanted to turn back when they had not walked more than a few kilometres. But Denny was firm. He made Andrew walk 12 kilometres; and on the next day he increased the distance to 15. By the end of the week they were walking 20 kilometres a day.

They did not speak during their walks. At first Andrew did not notice the beauty of the country; but gradually he began to enjoy the woods and rivers and mountains. The exercise and fresh air made him feel better. He began to eat and to sleep well. He even began to talk again. At first he made only an occasional remark. Then one day he asked Denny to tell him his news.

Denny had been waiting for this moment. 'Hope and I are both free men now. We've both given up our posts,' he told Andrew.

Andrew's face lit up. 'Given up? Then this means that we ...'
Denny smiled.

'I shall be fit to work again very soon,' Andrew said.

That evening, Denny and he looked at a map and made a list

of possible towns in which to start their new practice. A few days later, to Andrew's surprise, Hope arrived to join in the discussions. He made his usual jokes, and Andrew actually laughed.

'Of course,' said Denny, 'we are all completely crazy! We haven't much money. And we shall probably quarrel. But somehow . . .'

'We shall probably murder each other!' said Hope, rising and stretching himself.

Hope left the next morning. After breakfast, Andrew went for a walk by himself. It was good to feel fit again! He was looking forward to working with Denny and Hope. Yes, he really wanted to work again!

When he returned at 11 o'clock, he found two letters waiting for him. He sat beside Denny, who was reading the newspaper, and opened them.

One letter was from Mary Boland. She sent him her sympathy over Christine's death; told him that she herself was quite well again; and thanked him for everything that he had done for her.

Smiling, Andrew put down her letter, and read the other one. At once the smile left his face. He turned white. For a minute he sat quite still, looking at the letter.

'Denny,' he said in a quiet voice. 'Read this!'

Chapter 38   Andrew In Trouble

Eight weeks before, on her return from Stillman's hospital, Nurse Sharp had gone straight to see her friend, Nurse Trent, who was employed by Dr Hamson. They had arranged to go to the theatre together that evening. 'I'm sorry that I'm so late,' she cried. 'But Dr Manson has–'

At that moment, Hamson had come down the stairs. 'Hullo,

Nurse Sharp!' he said cheerfully. 'You look tired! And why are you both here so late? I thought that you were going to the theatre tonight.'

'Yes, Doctor,' said Nurse Sharp. 'But – I was delayed by Dr Manson.' She thought for a moment, and then decided to tell him the facts. 'Dr Manson took a girl away from the Victoria Hospital and drove her to that place in the Chilterns – to that new hospital, run by an American who is not a qualified doctor.' She told him the whole story.

There was a silence when she finished.

'I am sorry that you have had such a bad time, Nurse,' Freddie said, finally. 'Now, you had better hurry, or you will be late for the theatre.'

Freddie drove straight to his club to have dinner with Deedman and Ivory, with whom, since his quarrel with Andrew, he was now friendly again. During the meal, Freddie remarked: 'Manson seems to be taking some risks since he left us! I hear that he is sending patients to that man Stillman!'

'What!' Ivory almost shouted.

'Yes! And I understand that he also helped Stillman at an operation! His own nurse told me so.'

Ivory looked down at his plate and ate his dinner. He had not forgiven Manson for his remarks about the Vidler operation. Ivory knew that he was a bad surgeon. But nobody else had dared to tell him so! He hated Manson for that bitter truth.

After a few moments, he raised his head and said: 'We must do something about this! We must tell Gadsby. Gadsby spoke to me about Stillman the other evening. He had read a piece in a newspaper praising Stillman's work, and he was very angry. Gadsby is the man to tell.'

Hamson felt awkward. He did not want to get Manson into trouble. In a strange way, he quite liked Andrew. He said: 'Don't mention my name to Dr Gadsby!'

'Don't be a fool, Freddie! We can't allow Manson to behave like this!'

After dinner, Ivory went to see Dr Gadsby, who listened with interest to his story.

'Well! Well!' he said. 'I know this man Manson. He worked for the Coal and Mines Board. I didn't like him. He's a very unpleasant man! And you say that he actually took a patient from the Victoria and sent her to Stillman's place!'

'Yes – and he helped at the operation!'

'Then we must report the matter to the General Medical Council,' said Gadsby. 'I will report the matter personally. I consider this my duty. This man Stillman is a danger to the profession! If Manson has been working with him, he must not be allowed to practise – he must be disqualified.'

While Andrew was in Wales, he was reported, without his knowledge, to the General Medical Council. After taking statements from Dr Thoroughgood, Nurse Sharp, and one or two other people, the Council decided to hold an inquiry to consider the complaints against Andrew.

The letter which he now held in his hand gave Andrew notice of this decision.

Chapter 39 The Inquiry

A week before the inquiry, Andrew went to London to make arrangements for his defence. He was alone: he had told Denny and Hope that he would prefer to be alone. He felt very miserable. He could not believe that he, Andrew Manson, was in this situation – a situation which every doctor feared. Why should the Council wish to disqualify him from practising? He had done nothing shameful! In fact, he had done something that deserved praise: he had cured Mary Boland!

A lawyer named Hopper, suggested by Denny, agreed to defend Andrew at the inquiry. Andrew considered Hopper a weak, stupid man, and they nearly had a quarrel at their first meeting. Andrew wanted to ask Sir Robert Abbey, his only influential friend in London, to help him, but Hopper objected to this because Abbey was a member of the General Medical Council. The lawyer also refused to allow Andrew to call Stillman as a witness, because he was afraid that Stillman's presence might anger the members of the Council.

'What does that matter?' Andrew cried. 'I haven't done anything wrong! I'm not ashamed of my actions! I want the Council to know the truth. I want to prove to them that I saved this girl's life by sending her to Stillman – that my action was right and wise.'

'Dr Manson,' Hopper cried, 'I warn you not to talk like that at the inquiry! If you address the Council in that manner, they will certainly disqualify you! I advise you to say as little as possible. Simply answer their questions.'

Andrew realized that he must try to control his feelings.

On the evening before the inquiry, while out for a walk, Andrew came to the open doorway of a church. He entered. It was dark inside. He sat down in the back seat, and remembered how Christine used to read a prayer book when she was unhappy. He rarely went to church, but now here he was, like a man resting at the end of a journey. He prayed in silence: 'God, don't let them disqualify me! Don't let them disqualify me!' He remained there for perhaps half an hour. Then he rose and went to his hotel.

Next morning, he woke feeling sick with anxiety. He ate no breakfast. His case was to be heard at 11 o'clock, and Hopper had told him to arrive early.

He reached the offices of the General Medical Council as the clock was striking eleven.

He hurried along to the room where the inquiry was to be held. The members of the Council were sitting at a long table and at the far end of the room were the lawyers and witnesses who were to take part in the case. Mary Boland and her father, Nurse Sharp, Dr Thoroughgood, and several other faces that he recognized were there. Andrew stood for a minute, looking at the long line of chairs, and then sat down beside Hopper.

'I thought that I told you to be early,' the lawyer said.

Andrew did not answer.

The inquiry began immediately. Mr Boon, the lawyer employed by the doctors taking the action against Andrew, read out the charge against him. 'Mr President, gentlemen,' he said, 'this is a case of a doctor working with a person who is not qualified. The facts of the case are these. The patient, Mary Boland, was admitted to the Victoria Chest Hospital, on 18 July. She remained there, in the care of Dr Thoroughgood, until 14 September. She then expressed a wish to leave and return home. But, instead of returning home, the patient was taken by Dr Manson to a health centre run by a man named Stillman – a person not qualified in medicine and, er, a foreigner! Mr Stillman examined the patient as soon as she arrived and decided to operate at once on one of her lungs – and Dr Manson agreed to help him. They did the operation together. Gentlemen, I repeat: *they worked together!*'

Mr Boon looked at the members of the Council to make sure that they had understood his meaning, and then called for Dr Thoroughgood.

'Dr Thoroughgood,' he asked, 'is it true that Dr Manson came to the Victoria Hospital and requested you to change the treatment for this patient, Mary Boland?'

'Yes.'

'And what did you say?'

'I refused.'

'In the interest of your patient, you refused.'

'I did.'

'Was Dr Manson's manner strange when you refused?'

'Well . . .' Thoroughgood paused. 'He didn't seem to be very well that morning. He argued.'

'Thank you, Dr Thoroughgood. Had you any reason to believe that the patient herself was not satisfied?'

'Oh, no! She always seemed happy.'

'Thank you, Dr Thoroughgood. That is all.'

Boon questioned a nurse from the Victoria Hospital, and then called for Nurse Sharp.

'And now, Nurse Sharp, can you tell us about Dr Manson's actions on the afternoon of Wednesday, 14 September?'

'Yes, I was there!'

'I imagine from your voice, Nurse Sharp, that you did not wish to be there.'

'When I realized where we were going, and that this man Stillman is not a doctor, I was . . .'

'Disgusted?' Boon suggested.

'Yes, I was!'

'Exactly!' Boon looked pleased. 'And now, Nurse Sharp, one more question: did Dr Manson actually help Mr Stillman with this operation?'

'He did,' Nurse Sharp answered in a voice full of hate.

Abbey now leaned forward and asked a question. 'Is it a fact, Nurse Sharp, that Dr Manson had just given you notice?'

Nurse Sharp reddened. 'Yes. Yes – I suppose so.'

As she sat down, Andrew felt that Abbey, at least, was still his friend.

Boon, who was a little annoyed at this interruption, turned to the members of the Council: 'Mr President, gentlemen, I could call more witnesses, but I do not consider this necessary. I think that I have proved the charge against Dr Manson to be true.'

Mr Boon sat down, looking extremely pleased with himself. There was a moment's silence. Andrew kept his eyes on the floor. Bitterly, he told himself that they were treating him like a criminal. Then his own lawyer began to address the Council.

Hopper seemed awkward. His face was red, and he began to cough. He said: 'I admit the truth of this charge. But my friend Mr Boon was not quite fair to Dr Manson. He did not mention that Miss Boland was Dr Manson's own patient before she was in the care of Dr Thoroughgood. Dr Manson had a special interest in this case. I admit that Dr Manson's action in taking her away from the Victoria Hospital was quite wrong. But he was not dishonourable, and he certainly had no wish to offend against the medical laws. He did not agree with Dr Thoroughgood's treatment, and therefore decided to make other arrangements for the care of his patient.'

Hopper then called Mary Boland.

'Miss Boland,' he asked, 'did you find any cause of complaint while you were at Mr Stillman's hospital?'

'Oh, no! Certainly not!'

'Your health didn't get worse?'

'No, no – I got much better!'

'Thank you. That is all,' Hopper said quickly. 'I will now call Dr Manson.'

Andrew stood up, conscious that every eye was directed towards him. He was pale and tired.

Hopper addressed him. 'Dr Manson, did you receive any money from Mr Stillman?'

'None!'

'Did you intend to do harm to Dr Thoroughgood by your actions?'

'No – certainly not! We were good friends. I simply did not agree with his opinions about this case.'

'Exactly! You can tell the Council honestly that you did not mean to offend against the medical laws?'

'That is the truth.'

Hopper, who had worried about calling Andrew as a witness in case he should say too much, dismissed him with a feeling of relief.

Then Boon suddenly jumped to his feet and began to question Andrew. 'Dr Manson, you say that you did not mean to offend against the medical laws. But you knew that Mr Stillman was not qualified, didn't you?'

Andrew looked at him coldly. 'Yes, I knew that he was not a doctor.'

'I see! And that didn't stop you from sending a patient to him!'

'No – it did not!' Andrew was angry. He took a deep breath. 'Mr Boon, I've listened to you asking questions. Now I will ask you one. Have you heard of Louis Pasteur?'

Boon was surprised at the question. 'Yes – of course! Everyone has heard of him!'

'Exactly! Everyone has heard of him! Well, Mr Boon, do you realize that Louis Pasteur, the greatest name in scientific medicine, was not a doctor? Nor were many other famous names in medicine. Perhaps this will show you that every man who hasn't got a medical degree isn't necessarily a criminal or a fool!'

Silence! Every member of the Council sat up. Abbey looked at Andrew with a friendly expression. Hopper looked embarrassed. Boon was annoyed.

'Yes, yes – but those men had rare qualities,' said Boon. 'Surely you don't compare Stillman with them?'

'Why not? Those men had a long struggle before they became famous. Stillman has done more for medicine than thousands of men with degrees – far more than these doctors who drive about in expensive cars and charge high prices for their services! Stillman is a great man. He's done more for the cure of tuberculosis than any doctor in this country!'

His words caused surprise throughout the courtroom. Mary Boland looked at him with admiration. Hopper slowly and sadly began to put away his papers, feeling certain that Andrew had lost his case.

The President spoke. 'Do you really mean what you are saying, Dr Manson?'

'I do,' Andrew said firmly. He was determined to express his opinions. If they were going to disqualify him, he would give them cause to do so!

He continued: 'There are a great many things wrong with our profession, and it's time that we tried to correct them. Doctors are not trained properly. They learn only the basis of medicine at the medical schools. When I qualified, I was a danger to society. I only knew the names of a few diseases and the medicines that were supposed to cure them. I've learned nearly everything that I now know about medicine since I left medical school. But how many doctors study when they are running a practice? Very few! They are too busy to study. Our whole system is rotten! Doctors should work together and share their knowledge – make a real study of the causes and cures of their patients' diseases, instead of just giving bottles of medicine. What's happening now? Many doctors make fortunes from their patients by giving them medicines and expensive treatments that are useless! It isn't right! It isn't honest! I have made many mistakes myself, and I am sorry about them. But I made no mistake about Stillman, and I was right to turn to him. I ask you to look at Mary Boland. When she went to Stillman, she was dangerously ill. Now she's cured. Judge my actions by that!'

Andrew sat down.

For a minute there was silence. Then the President ordered everyone to leave the room.

Andrew went out with the others. He now felt angry with

himself. He wished that he had controlled his feelings, and had not spoken in that manner. He wanted so much to work with Denny and Hope. But now they would disqualify him!

The sound of people moving brought him to himself again. He joined the others and returned to the Council room. He sat quite still, his heart beating fast.

The President spoke. 'Andrew Manson, the Council has carefully considered the charge brought against you, and has decided to allow you to continue to practise medicine.'

For a moment Andrew hardly understood his words. Then his heart beat still faster with joy and relief. They had not disqualified him! He was free! He raised his head and looked at the members of the Council. Of all the faces that were turned towards him, the one that he saw most clearly was the face of Robert Abbey. At once he realized that it was Abbey who had saved him. He addressed the President, but it was to Abbey that he really spoke: 'Thank you, sir.'

Then his friends – Con, Mary, the surprised Mr Hopper, and people whom he had never seen before – came up to him and shook his hand. Mary, whose eyes were filled with tears, said: 'If they had disqualified you, after all that you have done for me, I'd – I'd have killed that old President!'

Andrew smiled.

The three – Andrew, Con and Mary – went to Andrew's hotel. There, waiting for them, was Denny. He walked towards them, smiling. Hopper had telephoned the news to him, but he did not mention this. He said simply: 'I'm hungry. Let's have lunch.'

Denny did not say a single word about the inquiry during lunch. After the meal, he told Andrew: 'We can buy that house that we want for our practice. It's quite cheap! Hope has gone to see it. Our train leaves at four o'clock. I must do some shopping now. I'll meet you at the station.'

Andrew looked at Denny, thinking of their friendship and of

all that he owed to him since their first meeting in the little Drineffy surgery. He said suddenly: 'What would have happened if they had disqualified me?'

'They didn't disqualify you!' Philip shook his head. 'And I will make sure that they never do.'

When Denny, Con and Mary had left, Andrew went to the churchyard where Christine was buried and stood for a long time by her grave. It was a bright, fresh afternoon – the sort of weather that she had always loved. When at last he turned away, hurrying for fear that he might be late, there in the sky before him a bank of cloud lay brightly, bearing the shape of battlements.

ACTIVITIES

Chapters 1–7

Before you read

1 The story is about a young doctor starting his first job. What problems do you think he will face?

2 Find these words in your dictionary. Remember that some words can have more than one meaning.

bacteria   carriage   hormone   microscope   misery
qualify   scorn   sewer   surgery   suspicion   typhoid

Mark each statement T (true) or F (false).

___ a *Bacteria* are alive.

___ b Before cars were common, many people travelled in *carriages*.

___ c You can order a *hormone* in a restaurant.

___ d *Microscopes* are useful to scientists.

___ e People are always full of *misery* when they win a great prize.

___ f Teachers must be *qualified* drivers.

___ g Teenagers are often *scornful* of advice from adults.

___ h *Sewers* are part of the electrical system of a modern city.

___ i You can visit an architect in his or her *surgery*.

___ j Detectives are good at examining people's *suspicions*.

___ k *Typhoid* fever is caused by a type of plant.

3 A *citadel* is a place where something that is important to you is kept safe and looked after. Name some professions that involve looking after people.

After you read

4 Which of the characters in the story:

a is Andrew's employer?

b is working for Dr Nicholls?

c is Andrew's first patient?

d destroy the local sewer?

e is the local schoolteacher?

f does Andrew save from a mental institution?

g studied with Andrew at university?

h is Andrew falling in love with?

5 What are the causes of Andrew's two quarrels with Christine? What arguments does each of them use in each case?

6 Discuss which of the doctors in the story you would be happy to ask for treatment. Explain why you would not visit the others.

Chapters 8–15

Before you read

7 What is the medical system in this South Wales town? What are its strengths and weaknesses?

8 Look these words up in your dictionary:

aneurism   experiment   research

a Which word means:

(i) a scientific test?

(ii) a lengthy study of a subject?

(iii) a medical problem?

b Complete each sentence with one of the new words.

(i) Marie Curie was famous for her important .... in the field of chemistry.

(ii) The science students perform a different .... each week.

(iii) The young man died suddenly of an ....

After you read

9 Who makes each of these remarks? What are they talking about?

a 'It's – it's come to life!'

b 'You consider only your own interests.'

c 'A house is provided.'

d 'What's your name, love?'

e 'My card, please, Doctor.'

f 'He's lost the use of his arm . . .'

g 'I'm just a jealous fool!'

h 'We must refuse to pay.'

10 Explain why Andrew:

   a decides to leave his first post.

   b is given the job in Aberalaw in spite of his lack of local experience.

   c becomes unpopular in Aberalaw.

   d decides to begin studying again.

11 Compare the characters and lives of Andrew Manson and Philip Denny. Explain why you think Andrew likes Philip.

12 Find the words in *italics* in your dictionary. Answer these questions:

   a If you *creep* into a room, how much noise do you make?

   b If you feel *relief*, are you probably happy or sad?

Chapters 16–23

Before you read

13 Look at the titles of the next few chapters. What do you think the answers are to the questions?

   Accident at the Mine

   a What exactly has happened at the mine?

   b How will Andrew be able to help?

   Christmas

   c Will Andrew and Christine enjoy their first Christmas in Aberalaw?

   The Rotten Bridge

   d Where is the rotten bridge?

   e What happens as a result of the bridge being rotten?

   Experiments

   f What is the purpose of Andrew's experiments?

   g What does he need to experiment on?

   An Offer of Work

   h What kind of job will Andrew be prepared to accept?

   The Coal and Mines Board

   i What are the responsibilities of the Board?

   Measuring Bandages

   j Why is Andrew involved in this work?

   k Will he enjoy it?

Andrew's First Practice
l What problems will Andrew face when he starts practising alone
in a new place?

After you read
14 Look back at the questions in Activity 13. What are the correct
answers? How many did you guess correctly?
15 Work in pairs and take the parts of Andrew and Christine. Tell each
other how you heard about the accident in the mine, what you did
and how you felt during the experience.
16 Discuss your feelings about medical experiments on animals.
Should they be allowed? What are the alternatives?

Chapters 24–31

Before you read
17 Will Andrew make a success of his practice? If so, how will he do
this? If not, what will the result be?
18 Answer these questions. Find the words in *italics* in your dictionary.
   a Where are your *tonsils*?
   b What are the effects of *hay fever*?
   c Do people suffer from *tuberculosis* in your country?

After you read
19 Answer the questions.
   a How has Freddie Hamson become rich?
   b Why is Andrew happy to accept Miss Everett as a patient?
   c Why are new clothes and a car so important to Andrew?
   d How does Andrew ask Christine to help in the surgery and why?
   e What lie did Andrew tell Christine?
   f Why does Andrew rent a room in the West End of London?
   g What happens in Andrew's love life while Christine is away?
   f What medical problem does Mary Boland have and how does
   Andrew help?
20 Who says this to Christine and why?
   'Don't worry about Andrew. But we must try to lead him back to his
   old Drineffy standards, mustn't we?'

21 Describe what you know about Stillman's background, his reason for coming to England and English doctors' views of him.

Chapters 32–39

Before you read

22 How do you think the story will develop in these areas? Give reasons for your opinions.
  a Andrew and Christine's marriage
  b Mary's operation
  c Andrew's relationship with Denny and Hope

23 Find these words in your dictionary:
  surgeon   battlements
  a Where does a *surgeon* work?
  b What does a *surgeon* do?
  c Where could you see *battlements*?
  d Why were they built originally?

After you read

24 Correct these statements if you think they are false.
  a Ivory is an experienced surgeon.
  b Harry Vidler dies from the shock of the operation.
  c Andrew stops giving medicines to patients who are not really ill.
  d Andrew is happy about Dr Thoroughgood's treatment of Mary Boland.
  e Stillman succeeds in curing Mary.
  f Christine is hit by a car and dies.

25 Why is Andrew reported to the General Medical Council? Who speaks against him at the hearing? What is the Council's decision?

26 Look back at the answers you gave in Activity 22. Were your guesses correct?

27 Describe the events leading to Christine's death and Andrew's feelings afterwards.

28 Work in pairs. Act out the arguments made against and in support of Andrew at the General Medical Council hearing.

29 Summarize Andrew's story in your own words, beginning from the time he became a doctor.

30 Discuss why you think the book is called *The Citadel*.

Writing

31 'There are a great many things wrong with our profession, and it's time we tried to correct them.' Describe what Andrew feels is wrong with the medical profession, as it was in the 1930s, and give examples from the story.

32 How much influence does Christine have over Andrew? Describe the points in the story where you feel her influence was most important.

33 Imagine you are Andrew. Write a letter to Abbey after the General Medical Council hearing. Thank him for his support and tell him about your plans for the future.

34 You are a newspaper reporter. Write about Andrew's case at the General Medical Council.

35 You are Mary Boland. Write to Andrew just after his wife's death. Thank him for all he has done and say how sorry you were to learn of Christine's death.

36 Do you think the pictures painted of doctors in the book are believable? Discuss any differences between the medical systems in the story and those in place in your country today.